Black Cherries

Grace Stone Coates

Introduction to the Bison Books Edition by
Mary Clearman Blew

University of Nebraska Press
Lincoln and London

First Nebraska paperback printing: 2003

For permission to reprint certain of these stories, the author's thanks are due to H. G. Merriam, editor of *The Frontier*, and John T. Frederick, editor of *The Midland*.

Library of Congress Cataloging-in-Publication Data
Coates, Grace Stone, 1881–1976.
Black cherries / by Grace Stone Coates; introduction to the Bison edition by Mary Clearman Blew.
p. cm.
ISBN 0-8032-6429-1 (pbk.: alk. paper)
1. Problem families—Fiction. 2. Rural families—Fiction. 3. Poor families—Fiction.
4. Farm life—Fiction. 5. Kansas—Fiction. 6. Girls—Fiction. I. Title.
PS3505.O1325B58 2003
813'.54—dc21 2002028527

To
HENDERSON

Contents

MARY CLEARMAN BLEW

Introduction

Considering the explosion of interest during the last thirty years in the literature of the American West, the accumulated wealth of critical and scholarly material on that literature, and, in particular, the popularity currently enjoyed by the writers of Montana, it seems distinctly odd to be introducing a collection of prize-winning short fiction written in Montana by a woman whose name has been forgotten by everyone except for a handful of local bookworms and John Updike, who chose her story "Wild Plums" to represent 1929 in *Best American Short Stories of the Century*.[1]

Although I grew up in Montana and, during my high school years, read every book I could find in our little Carnegie library by a Montana writer—B. M. Bower, A. B. Guthrie Jr., Joseph Kinsey Howard, Dorothy Johnson, Frank Linderman, Mildred Walker—I had never heard of Grace Stone Coates until, in 1982, while serving on the editorial board of what would become *The Last Best Place: A Montana Anthology*,[2] I was introduced to Coates's poetry and fiction by the late Richard Roeder, then a professor of history at Montana State University in Bozeman. Rich had been researching homestead reminiscences and had set himself the goal of finding every memoir written by settlers of the Montana homestead frontier, many of which had been privately printed and privately circulated. When he came across Grace Stone Coates, he was amazed—"She was cited more times in *Best American Short Stories* than any other writer before or since," he told me; and, indeed, whether or not it is a record, twenty of her short stories were cited by series editor Edward J. O'Brien in the annual *Best American Short Stories* as Distinctive or Honor Roll stories during a single seven-year period.[3] The story that O'Brien chose for 1929, "Wild Plums," was also the story chosen by John Updike for *Best American Short Stories of the Century*. During that same period, from the late 1920s through the early 1930s, Coates's poetry was appearing in magazines as well known as *American Mercury* and *Poetry*. The Caxton Printers of Idaho published two collections of her poems, *Mead and Mangel-Wurzel* in 1931 and *Portulacas in the Wheat* in 1932, and *Black Cherries* was published in 1931 by Alfred A. Knopf.[4]

Then, abruptly, Grace Stone Coates ceased writing. No one knows why. Her last published short story appeared in the summer edition of *The Frontier* in 1935. At that time she was fifty-four years old. She lived to be ninety-five. Her biography had appeared in *Who's Who in America* and *Principal Women in America* in 1935, but by the time of her death in a Bozeman, Montana, nursing home in 1976, she had been so completely forgotten that no memorial service was held and no obituary appeared in local newspapers. All that saved her work from total oblivion was the friendship of a young woman named Lee Rostad, who, like Coates herself, had come to Martinsdale as a young bride with a college education. Lee Rostad visited the elderly Coates in her nursing home, listened to her reminiscences, collected what she could of her scattered papers, and eventually wrote her biography, which includes a number of Coates's poems.[5]

So who was Grace Stone Coates, whose writing received so much acclaim during such a brief period and then faded into obscurity? Why did she begin to write, and why did she stop writing? And what is it about her single collection of linked short stories—*Black Cherries*—that readers in the twenty-first century will find so vital and so compelling?

She was born Grace Stone on a wheat farm in Kansas in 1881 to Heinrich and Olive Sabrina Stone. Her childhood seems to have paralleled the childhood she depicts for her narrator, Genevieve (Veve) von S., in *Black Cherries*. Like Genevieve, Grace was her father's favorite daughter. Later she recalled long walks with him, listening to him recite poetry, and learning the names of trees and flowers from him. Life on the wheat farm was hard, however, and Heinrich Stone was a gambler who speculated on land, lost everything, and then recouped his losses with the invention of a flywheel for a binder. He sold his invention to a machinery company, went to work for the company as a salesman, and traveled extensively in the United States and abroad, while his family lived without him, first in Kansas City, later in Wisconsin, and then in Chicago, where Grace spent a year at the University of Chicago.

After her mother's death, Grace taught school. By 1910, she had followed her sister, Helen, west and was teaching high school in Butte, Montana, when she met and married Henderson Coates of Martinsdale, a tiny ranching community in southwestern Montana. She lived in Martinsdale, except for her final stay in the nursing home in Bozeman, for the rest of her life.[6]

In 1927 Grace Stone Coates became acquainted with H. G. Merriam, the legendary Rhodes scholar and professor of English who had founded the creative writing program at the University of Montana and was about to start a literary magazine, *The Frontier*, to encourage and publish the works of otherwise unknown writers in the Northwest. Apparently Merriam was struck by Grace Stone Coates's talent because almost immediately he asked her to work as a fiction editor on his fledgling magazine and to submit her own work. She was thrilled. "It is impossible for me to put on paper today the enthusiasm I feel about your new venture," she wrote. "When I offered to help, what I meant was to help the magazine, not help myself, as you have permitted me to do. Of course I'll undertake the work; and of course I'll send manuscripts as soon as possible."[7]

Thus began the seven-year burst of creative energy that generated the twenty citations in *Best American Short Stories*. Within a year Merriam was urging Coates to put together a collection of her "family" stories for submission to a New York editor. A few months later, he wrote, "Why not plan a *Novel* novel to be made up of about twenty short stories. . . . The tragedy or whatever you care to call it (you needn't stick to fact) of a second marriage [which] would come out thru the eyes, ears and sensibilities of the little girl. . . . Each story would be complete in itself, and yet bound with all the others thru the unfolding of the central story."[8]

And so Coates set to work revising the stories that would be published as *Black Cherries*. She immediately ran into difficulties: "I'm stuck but not discouraged," she wrote to Merriam during the winter of 1929. "In the first place the stories were written independently.... As I try to write toward them I get into straight novel material. If I'm writing a novel I might as well chuck these stories, and do it."[9]

Today it requires a wrench of perspective to think of a collection of short stories linked by character and place as *novel*, and yet in 1929 both Merriam and Coates saw *Black Cherries* as groundbreaking. The stories portray a tightly self-contained family held together by the almost unbearable tensions of half-understood secrets and resentments. The father, like Coates's own father, worships the memory of his dead first wife and uses his mordant wit to punish and control his second wife, while she, humorless and controlling in her own self-abnegating way, pines and dies from repeated miscarriages in her attempts to bear a son. Augusta and Carl, the two children from the first marriage, are beaten and humiliated by their father. Teressa, oldest of the two children from the second marriage, is turned into a weeping household drudge by the time she is ten. Only the narrator, little Veve, five years old when the book begins and twelve when it ends, experiences some of the pleasures of childhood as she plays and daydreams and tries to understand the unspoken edicts of her family.

Taken as a whole, *Black Cherries* tells of a child's awakening, not so much to sexuality itself, but to the ways in which the tensions of sexuality are destroying her family. The very titles of individual stories—"The Nymphs and Pan," "The Way of the Transgressor," "Late Fruit," "Wild Plums"—suggest the underlying themes of secret pleasures, rebellion, and guilt, which are developed through imagery of the natural world and the day-to-day trivia of farm life. "The Way of the Transgressor," for example, has to do with the mystery of the banished half-sister, Augusta, who had had the habit of taking the kitchen knives and hacking the blades until they had to be resharpened on the grinder.

Six-year-old Veve decides to try knife-hacking: "I wondered why Augusta hacked them, and why it was wrong. There was something dark and exciting about her doing it.... When I struck the blades together it made little pains run up and down my legs, as if it hurt the knives" (17). Her parents, discovering the ruined knives, ask Veve whether Augusta had showed her how. "Father's face looked thin and white. . . . He said, 'If I *knew* she did it to flout me, if I *knew* she did it in scorn of me, to fling back into my face the villainy of that infernal—'" (18).

The reader, seeing the scene through Veve's eyes, is almost as puzzled as she is. Who is the infernal one? Augusta, we must suppose. And what was her villainy, that caused her to be banished from the family at age twelve or so? We have no way of knowing, except what we might guess from the unexplained, terrible tension between Veve's mother and father and from the story's lush, oppressive imagery.

In another story, "Late Fruit," Veve doesn't understand that her mother is pregnant and plans to stay with an aunt while she gives birth. For reasons that Veve also doesn't understand, her mother and father discuss which of the children she will take with her: "If mother took me with her it would leave Teressa alone with father and the hired men. Sometimes mother said, *alone with Carl.* I did not know why Teressa could not stay alone with Carl. They did not quarrel. Carl told Teressa things the hired men told him, that neither of them would tell me" (21).

Eventually the mother takes Carl with her to the aunt's, leaving nine-year-old Teressa home to keep house for her father and take care of Veve. She is gone long enough that the peaches ripen and fall off the trees and are canned by Teressa, who has been kept home from school by her father in spite of his promises to her mother. Veve, worried by letters from her mother asking her to save some peaches for her, finds a late-ripening tree and collects eleven peaches, which she sets on a kitchen shelf. But her father eats every peach. And when her mother returns— the new baby apparently died at birth—she blames Veve for eating the peaches. "Something had happened while mother was away that she and father were not happy about, and eating the peaches seemed part of it. I hoped mother would tell me it was wrong for father to eat them. It seemed wrong. If it was wrong, and he did it, I would understand and not care" (26–27).

In a story called "The Flyleaf in the Book of Disillusion," we get our only real glimpse of Carl, the half-brother, as Veve observes Carl and Teressa playing their favorite game of Enchantment: "They stayed right by my side where they had been, but they couldn't speak and couldn't be seen. They had played this game all the morning. It bothered me a little, and made me feel queer, because I was afraid they were looking at what I was thinking. I watched things outside me and tried not to think" (36).

Veve yearns for a cottonwood blossom at the very top of a tree, thinking it an object of great beauty, indeed a fairy tassel: "I could not tell which was harder to bear, to see [the cottonwood blossoms] swing gently in the soft wind . . . or to watch them hang motionless, meaning something I could not understand. Motionless, they frightened me. . . . Dancing, they excited me beyond reason" (35–36). Carl finally understands how badly Veve wants the particular cottonwood blossom at the top of the tree and, with Teressa's reluctant assistance, climbs the cottonwood tree and brings back the blossom. At the sight of it in her hand, Veve bursts into tears, to the bewilderment of Carl. Wasn't it the blossom she wanted? Did she want a yellow one? A red one? But Veve only shakes her head, until Teressa becomes exasperated and urges the troubled Carl to run away with her and hide from Veve. "But I knew why I had cried," Veve ends the story, "though words to tell it were not yet mine. . . . I knew, once and for all, that fairy things against the sky fall humdrum, to be trampled under foot" (37).

As remarkable an achievement as *Black Cherries* seems today, its reception in 1931 was lukewarm. Its print run was small (the copy on my desk as I write has Grace Stone Coates's signature on the flyleaf and the notation that this is number 1486 of 1500 copies), and its reviews were mixed. Coates seems to have shrugged off some hostile comments about her book in Montana, but she responded enigmatically to a *New York Times* reviewer who suggested that as a full-fledged novel *Black Cherries* might have had a wider range and a more permanent value. "*Black Cherries* falls between two schools," Coates wrote. "It is more than a collection of stories, it is less than a novel. . . . If *Black Cherries* had not been written for publication, it would have been a more coherent book, save for one difficulty: for publication it would never have been written."[10]

Coates's last puzzling statement—"for publication it would never have been written"—suggests a level of her anger and frustration that is difficult to interpret. Given the highly autobiographical content of *Black Cherries*, and Merriam's hint—"you needn't stick to fact"—it is tempting to speculate that, for Coates, a more coherent book would have been a more revealing book than she would have felt she could publish. What might such a book have revealed? At this reach of time, we know only that *Black Cherries* depicts a family caught in a web of tension so acute that it binds them inexorably even as it separates them. Whatever we may guess about the banishment of Augusta, the half-veiled asides about Carl, the mother's endless series of miscarriages or stillbirths, and the punishing irony and controlling behavior of the father, we understand that this is a family in anguish. By the end of *Black Cherries*, everyone in the family except Veve and Teressa are alienated from one another.

After the publication of *Black Cherries*, an increasingly worried H. G. Merriam tried hard to get Coates to resume writing and submit a novel to Knopf. "If you are going to continue as a writer—and you must do so—it is time that another book by you should appear," he wrote to her in 1934.[11] She did have a large manuscript for a novel, Coates replied. "Your comment to Mr. Knopf moved me. . . . Oh, I have a glorious idea if it just works out."[12]

But either her idea didn't work out, or something within Coates wasn't working out. She made excuses to Merriam—she pleaded her garden, she pleaded her local commitments—but gradually their warm friendship seemed to cool, and their correspondence slowed. Perhaps she sensed in Merriam a tendency for control; perhaps she was unwilling to face any more of her grim past. Whatever the explanation, she continued to encourage and assist other writers. She advised Frank Linderman, Taylor Gordon, Gwendolyn Haste, and William Saroyan, among others. She did some feature writing for local newspapers, but her literary career was done. After a final story, which appeared in the summer 1935 issue of *The Frontier*, she never published another line of fiction.[13]

The story of Grace Stone Coates's life may or may not be read as a writer's cautionary tale: *what happens when we don't face our demons*. But the artistry of *Black Cherries* remains, thanks to friends like Lee Rostad and Richard Roeder, who would not let it be forgotten, and the

University of Nebraska Press, which again makes it available to a wide audience.

NOTES

1. Grace Stone Coates, "Wild Plums," in *Best American Short Stories of the Century*, eds. John Updike and Katrina Kenison (Boston: Houghton Mifflin, 1999), 100–104.

2. *The Last Best Place: A Montana Anthology*, eds. William Kittredge and Annick Smith (Helena MT: Montana Historical Society Press, 1988).

3. Edward J. O'Brien, ser. ed., *Best American Short Stories* (Boston: Houghton Mifflin, 1915–41).

4. Richard Roeder, "Grace Stone Coates, Forgotten Poet and Writer," circa 1985, unpublished essay, in the collection of Lee Rostad.

5. Lee Rostad, *Grace Stone Coates: Honey Wine and Hunger Root* (Helena MT: Falcon, 1985).

6. Rostad, *Honey Wine*, 95–96.

7. Coates to Merriam, July 1929, in the collection of Lee Rostad.

8. Merriam to Coates, December 1928, in the collection of Lee Rostad.

9. Coates to Merriam, n.d., in the collection of Lee Rostad.

10. Coates, "Black Cherries and Spinach," *Contempo: A Review of Ideas and Personalities*, I, 6 (mid-July 1931), 2.

11. Merriam to Coates, 9 September 1934, Merriam Papers, University of Montana, Box 18, Folder 18.

12. Coates to Merriam, n.d., in the collection of Lee Rostad.

13. Coates, "Far Back, Far Forward," *The Frontier: A Magazine of the West* (summer 1935), 299–303.

BLACK CHERRIES

Crickets

I lay on the floor by my father. I could have gone to my sister's bed, and she would have grumbled and cuddled me up, and let me curl my hands in her soft neck. I could have gone to mother, who would have chided me soberly, and taken me in; but I lay on the floor with my father. He was very long, lying there, and incredibly old. Mother had told me at the last birthday cake that he was forty-nine. I was almost five.

There were times in summer, when he had been shoveling wheat all day, or cold-hammering plowshares at the end of every double furrow, that father would come in after all the night chores were done, pull a big white sheet out of the linen drawer, spread it by the open door, and lie down. Mother would say, "Oh, Henry, *please* don't do that. *Please* undress and make yourself comfortable and go to bed." He would answer, "Yes, yes!"—but it didn't mean *yes*; it meant not to talk any more. He would lie with his hands clasped under his head, and stare at the ceiling, and I would slip down beside him. The brussels carpet pricked a little, through the sheet and my thin nightdress.

Father didn't notice what I said to him. I liked to be with him when he was thinking, because I could say a great many things one didn't say to persons who listened too hard, like mothers. I could use words that didn't really belong to me, words in books, if I said them softly. If I said them in the daytime, in front of my sister Teressa, her stocky legs would scamper to mother, and she would pant excitedly, "Mother, mother! Veve is putting on!" She would look over her shoulder at me while she talked.

Lying by father, I could whisper words like *valley, daisy, fern*. I had never seen a fern, except a brittle one in mother's Bible. It always broke a little, no matter how gently I looked at it. I had never seen valleys, but I knew how they would look, rich and dark.

Father liked the hardness of the floor, except that it hurt his bones when he was lean in summer. As I lay beside him I could smell the new cloth in his shirt. Mother had finished making the shirt the day before. I could smell the wire of the screen door, and a little carpety smell through the sheet. Mosquitoes unwound a sharp song outside the door, and moths bumped into its mesh with soft thuds. A fly, caught in a crevice, annoyed my father, and he shook the screen to stop its buzzing. I wondered why flies bothered him. I liked them; they always seemed in earnest.

After I had lain on the floor for a time, an insect began to sing beyond the open door. LOUD and *soft*, LOUD and *soft*, it sang, with one little jetting spurt of shrill music at regular intervals. It was something that sang often but not always. It sang when everything was quiet, and I listened hard. I knew it was a cricket. It had to be a cricket. I asked my father; but though he raised his head to listen, he said he couldn't hear it. I wondered if he knew about crickets . . . lively as a cricket. . . . The Cricket on the Hearth . . . cricket-bats. . . . I wondered if he had ever seen a cricket. I hadn't. I asked him again what it was that was singing, and he listened again, and said the noise was quite possibly subjective— which was just like saying nothing. I felt shut up inside myself because he didn't tell me. I shook his arm, a soft shake, and asked him, "What would it be, even if you don't hear it? What would it be?"

He raised his head slightly, and slanted his gaze mildly toward me along his bended elbow: "Some of the nocturnal stridulating Gryllidæ, I assume."

His words sounded like bells. Like church bells. I said them over and over to myself. I had never heard church bells. I had never been to church, except Sunday school in the schoolhouse. Because Mrs. Slump nursed her baby in Sunday school, father called her a sow. I was glad he had said church bells instead of saying grasshoppers. Grasshoppers made me think of sunshine, and the hot, dusty smell of grain shocks. But this sound was cool, like dark night odors close to the ground.

Always the song went on.

Mother came to the door of her bedroom, braiding her hair over her shoulder. She looked worried. She glanced at me, and said, "You should be asleep." I wrinkled my eyes tight shut and said, "I am." When I opened them she smiled, but she was frowning, too. Father put his arm over me. He didn't say, "Let the child stay," but that was what he meant. The last thing I remembered was mother standing beside the door looking at us, braiding her dark hair and frowning a little.

The Nymphs and Pan

It made mother uncomfortable when I looked steadily at the picture in her bedroom. I studied it longer to find out why. Looking at it was like doing other things she told me not to. I wondered why I shouldn't, and thought about it until I did them to find out. Sometimes I learned only that I mustn't.

The things father told me were different. He told me not to hide in the standing wheat ahead of the binder, because I might fall asleep, and the sickle strike me before he saw me; or I might frighten the horses until he could not control them. He told me not to stand on a wagon wheel after the team was hitched up, because if the horses started I might be caught in the wheel and dragged; and not to feed the mother pigs to keep them from looking at me, because he was saving the corn I had been giving them for a different purpose.

The picture in mother's room hung above a chair. The chair was heavier than I could move, and was not cane-seated, so I could stand in it without hurting it. Mother didn't tell me not to look at the picture, she told me not stand in the chair. I needed to look harder, after that, because I had to be farther away.

I thought it was a picture from the Bible until father explained it to me. He said it was a steel engraving. It was a picture of *Nymphs and Pan*. Two nymphs were trying to pull Pan into a pool of water. Each had hold of one of his hands, and all three were laughing. The whole picture was fun. I felt sure the nymphs couldn't pull him in unless he wanted them to. He braced his hoofs, and drew them toward him. The upper part of him was a man, and the lower part a goat. His hair was little curls. Father said the picture was a pagan conception of joyousness, and to think it not beautiful was vulgar.

I liked to look at it, because things in it seemed more *so* to me than if they had been real. The grass was like other grass than itself, and made me think of places I knew, and places I only imagined. The water was sunny, and if one were there things would not be different than one knew they were going to be. I could think of the people in the picture as if they were moving. Pan could have put the nymphs in the water if he had wanted to. It would not have been impolite, for the day looked warm, and none of them had clothes on.

There was something I played outdoors that made me think of the picture. It made me feel the way the nymphs and Pan looked, as if I were having a good time. I tied a long piece of binding twine around my waist behind, so one end had to follow me when I walked. It was interesting to think it had to go every place I did. When I walked, it couldn't stop; and when I stopped, it couldn't go. Even if it took hold of something, unless I waited for it, it couldn't stay. I tried to think of some way to make little hands for it to catch hold of weeds with, but I couldn't think of any.

One day I had played with it a long time. I had gone the hardest places for it I could think of. I had walked on plowed ground, and over the cob pile, and through a thistle patch, to make it have to follow me. It seemed as though I would be more rested if everything were not so still around me. I wanted something to make sound while I walked. I thought I knew how I could fasten a pan in front of me for a drum. We had big pans for milk, and a little pan for other things, that mother liked best. I went to the house to see if mother was asleep, so I could take one without bothering her; but she was awake. She was in the pantry making cookies. We were not allowed to ask twice for the same thing, so I thought it would be best to ask first for a big pan, and then for the little one.

After I had asked mother for the milk pan, and told her why I wanted it, she said, "Certainly not," so I asked for the small pan. She said, "Certainly not," harder than before. "You know better than to tease for a thing after I have said, 'No.'" I tried to explain that I was asking about different pans, but mother did not like to have children argue.

I went outdoors. I didn't put the string back on me, but sat under the edge of the east porch, in the shade.

Mother did not want us to ask "Why?" when she said, "No," so I waited until another time to find out why I couldn't have the pan. I asked her that night when she was putting me to bed. She said, "When I tell you you can not have a thing, that is reason enough, without your bothering me when I am tired."

I said, "If I ask you when you are rested will you tell me?"

I thought mother was going to shake me. She never spanked me, but she gave me shakings when I needed them. She had her hands on my shoulders, but unpressed her lips, and told me pans cost money, and were made to be used; they were not good to put milk in after they rocked on the bottom; and beating a pan would spoil it. I would have beaten one very gently if she had let me, or worn it and listened to it only with my mind.

I didn't tell mother this. I wanted first to see whether I could beat one without hurting it. I went to sleep thinking about the picture in her bedroom, because the people in it did what they were doing entirely, without having to make any part of it different.

Black Cherries

The black-cherry tree that stood beyond the kitchen door was mother's. At first, at the very earliest, I thought the tree *was* mother. I thought it was mother-being-a-tree. Later I thought it was a mother-tree. But my sister Teressa explained to me that it was mother's tree because she liked its sweet black cherries. She could not eat the sour pie-cherries we gobbled greedily. It was her tree.

Mother liked all trees, except the two palm-like strangers standing outside the pantry window. She loved trees, and the black-cherry best of all. Only by her permission could we break one splayed white blossom. For her we snapped bare winter twigs, with smooth dark ice-glazed bark. For her, in summer, we dug "gum," well bedded with ants and Kansas dust. There was a curious thing about our gifts of amber sap. Although I often stood at her side, for the vicarious rapture of seeing a bit of shiny "gum" slip between her lips, I could never catch the exact moment when she tasted the treasure. Always the fire needed attention, or a pail must be emptied. Once when I had brought her an unusually ample lump, I turned back at the door to reclaim a morsel for myself. She said it was all gone. I was puzzled. I was so puzzled I asked to look in her mouth. I thought there must be a small piece, somewhere, she didn't know she hadn't swallowed. Mother acted bothered. She said part of the gum had had bark on it, and she hadn't eaten that. After I went outdoors I wondered for a long time how she could swallow a sticky thing so quickly.

It was for mother we guarded the cherry tree's black fruit.

Because of something that happened, once, as I gathered her an offering, the tree stands forever in the disquieting twilight which haunts unhappy dreams—the shadow that prevents any dream from being happy.

It was the edge of evening, in the slow, long summer half-light. I was alone, peering into the branches of the tree, picking a cherry here and there. The season was almost over; little fruit was left. I held the cherries by their stems as I gathered them, making a tight bouquet. As I thought of mother taking them, I could feel her smooth fingers flatten against mine, transferring the cluster deftly to preserve its careful shape. Some of the cherries I touched slipped from their pits and smeared my fingers. These I ate. When I had pulled a branch down within reach, I would catch a twig in my teeth to hold it. The leaves brushed my face. The bark was pungent in my nostrils and on my tongue. I pretended I was part of the tree.

While I was looking into the branches' deepening blackness, mother came from the house with Teressa at her side. She held Teressa's hand, and that was queer; Teressa didn't like to be touched. I went toward them, offering mother my cherries. She pushed my hand away as if I were not there, and said, "Not now." Her face was white in the dusk. I looked at her and she said again, still as if I were not there, "I couldn't taste them. They would sicken me. Come, we are going for a walk."

She took my free hand, and still holding Teressa's, started across the yard. Suddenly she dropped our hands and turned back to the house, saying, "Stay there!" over her shoulder as she went. We waited. I rubbed the cherries up and down against my cheek. I knew this was not nice, but I did it anyway. I liked the way they felt. If doing it stayed in my mind and bothered me, I would rinse the cherries off at the pump before I gave them to mother. They felt like glass. I could smell them and make them smell like blossoms, or I could smell them and make them smell like bark. I told Teressa this, and she said, "I hate you."

It grew darker while mother was in the house. She came out of the kitchen door, walking fast. As she stepped from the low platform to the path, my oldest sister, Augusta, came running after her, crying, "Don't go! Don't go!"

Without turning her head, or stopping, mother said, "Go back,"

but Augusta ran around in front of her, crouched down, and caught
mother around the knees. She kept saying, "Please, please, please don't
leave me." I wondered why Augusta didn't go with us.

Mother did not move. She looked straight ahead and said, "Go back."
I saw the buttons on the back of Augusta's dress, and her bent head,
and the way her braids jerked when her shoulders shook. Augusta was
old. She was more than ten. She did not speak or cry on her way back
toward the house, but her shoulders went up and down.

Mother came toward us and took our hands. She almost ran. Usually
mother did not take short cuts, or climb fences. She went on paths. But
this time we went straight through the orchard without going by the
road. We went through deep grass, past sunflowers in the corner where
sand burrs grew, to the fence. It was a board fence. I hurried to get
through first, because I wanted to see how mother went through a fence
where there was no gate. I caught myself between two tight boards, and
when I could look again mother and Teressa were through. Past the
fence we were in a plowed field. We went so fast I had to take little
running steps to keep up. My fingers ached from holding the cherry
stems. It was strange to be walking fast and not talking. I wondered
why Augusta didn't want us to go, and why she had not come with us.
I asked. I knew it was naughty to ask. Mother's voice sounded far away.
She said Augusta had to study her lessons, and for me not to talk.

We walked a long time. I was tired. All at once mother turned around,
and leaving us both, began to run toward the house. It was like the
horrible queerness of a dream to see her running over the plowed ground
in the darkness. Teressa took my hand and we began to run, too. We
caught up with mother on the other side of the fence. I wondered again
whether she went between the boards or climbed over them. As we
came out of the orchard she looked over her shoulder and said, "Stay
back," just as she had before; only this time she said it to Teressa.

Teressa said we must go to the granary to gather eggs she had
forgotten. It took her a long time to look for them, and she didn't
find them.

When we came to the house there was a light in the kitchen. Father
was sitting at the table by my brother, teaching him square root. I knew
it was square root, because Carl was crying onto his slate. Mother went

through the kitchen with a washbasin in her hand, and a towel. She went to Augusta's room. When she came out I asked her if Augusta had a headache, and she said, "Yes. Keep out of her room."

Father and Carl had a worse and worse time. Father said, "I can make you see it with a strap." He said that whenever he taught Carl. Mother did something that seemed strange, as all the rest of the evening had been. I had never known her to help Carl, before, when father was teaching him. She said in a clear voice that sounded loud, "Carl, put up your books. Wash your face and go to bed." Carl looked at her with his mouth a little open. She said again, "Put away your books." His eyes were round, and he tiptoed when he crossed the room.

After he had gone, mother walked toward the porch door. A strap hung beside it, high on a nail. The strap was long, and had holes in one end. Mother took it down, and rolled it in her hands as she walked toward the stove. She was saying, "You shall never touch a child again, yours or mine, as long as I live in this house." She lifted the stove lid and put the strap on the coals.

I wondered why she said yours *or* mine.

She walked to the table where father sat. He did not look up. I could hear the air being still around her before she spoke. A small sharp singing began, that I could always hear when I listened hard, especially when I listened for something that had not happened yet. Mother said, "I will not live in a house where children are abused."

She turned and saw me. I had been sitting by the window, almost hidden by the curtain, and she had forgotten me. She told me sharply to go to bed, and added that I should have gone without telling, when Teressa did. I laid the cherries on the window sill. They lay there in the morning when I got up, tumbled on their heads. I did not eat them.

The next day I played alone all day. I knew things I had not known the morning before. There were things one learned, and things one knew without learning. Things I learned were like pictures to paste in a scrapbook. Things I knew were like pages to paste pictures on. I had learned that Augusta and Carl were not like Teressa and me. They were different the way things we bought were different from things we raised in the garden. What I knew was this: learning about one thing that puzzled me only made other things to wonder about. Why were Carl and Augusta different? Why did they cry when they studied? Why did father teach them, when mother always taught us? And why had the entire evening been so queer?

The questions came, and burrowed, and lay still, and wriggled again, always with the tickling brush of cherry leaves against my face, the scent and tang of cherry bark, and forbidden red-black smoothness across my cheek; always with the choking mystery of twilight, and the strangeness of plowed ground under hurrying feet.

The Way of the Transgressor

What made me remember things was that father and mother talked about them. One thing I did was like another, and I forgot it, unless they talked and made me remember. Once, mother left me alone to get dinner for father and the hired man; and once everybody left me. Both times things happened that people talked about until they stayed in my mind.

The first time mother left me, it was to take Teressa to the dentist. She thought it would be hard for me to get dinner, and told me how: to take one cup of rice and three cups of boiling water, with salt; and to begin to cook it at half-past eleven. She showed me how the hands of the clock would look at dinner time, and pinned a picture of it on the wall, with hands that way, so I wouldn't forget. I told her I knew when it was half-past eleven, but she made the picture anyway. I did know, except that I thought five minutes on the clock was one minute.

The rice was all I had to cook. Father liked rice, and the hired man could eat meat already prepared.

I set the table almost as soon as mother and Teressa left. I built a good fire. We burned cobs in summer time, and mother and Teressa always talked about keeping the kitchen cool and keeping the flies out. When the fire began to burn hard I went into the front room to look at books, but laid them down, often, to see what time it was. The fire went out twice before it was time to cook the rice, and I built it again.

When I measured the rice, one cup looked too little for two people. I thought mother might have said three cups of rice instead of three cups of water, so I measured out three. It was a good deal. It took more water than there was hot, so I put in cold. I put in salt, but not enough. After the rice began to boil I went into the front room again until father came to dinner. He came in ahead of the hired man, to see if I was getting along all right. I heard him come, so I went out before he could call me, and said I was. He said, "Gee Whillaker, it's hot!" I said, "Yes, isn't it? I was staying in the other room." Father laughed. He laughed all the time we were eating dinner. He had me bring a large plate to set under the butter dish, so the butter wouldn't drip on the tablecloth.

It was fun to sit in mother's place and ask to have things passed to me.

Dinner was so easy to get I would not have thought about it again, except that father told mother about it when she came home. He said, "The kitchen was an inferno, and the butter was swimming; but the cook sat cool and unconcerned in the parlor while the dinner cooked itself. She is of the earth, earthy."

Teressa heard him. She pinched me. She said, "Oh, it is sweet and wonderful when *you* let the butter melt, but if I do it, it's a crime." She pinched me more, and said, "How wonderful to be such a wonderful child, you little idiot!" Then she made me say I loved her, and held me on her lap and rocked me. She told me the poem:

See, by the moonlight 'tis past midnight,
Time kid and I were home an hour and a half ago.

I liked that one, because the way she said it made my chest shake.

The time mother and father left me entirely alone they talked about it three or four days before they went. I did not understand why they disliked to leave me. People were always inside themselves, anyway, and other persons outside them. It seemed almost the same whether they were outside close by, or outside farther off. I said this to mother, but she told me not to be silly.

Something happened this time they were away that they talked about until I cried.

Before they left mother said: "Be a good girl. When it is dinner time put the small tablecloth on the table, set it, and sit down to eat just as we always do; and be a good girl." Father told me things, too, but they were things not to do; funny things I couldn't have done anyway, like hiding the end of the road so they couldn't finish coming home. Mother didn't think they were funny. As father got into the buggy he said, "And don't hack the knives."

Mother said, "Don't be bitter, Henry. Those things are past."

Father said, "Nothing is ever past."

I knew what father meant about the knives. When Augusta was staying at home, before father sent her away to her grandmother, she hacked knives. Augusta was a very bad girl. At least, I had supposed she was bad; but when I said, "I hate Augusta," mother was angry. "Augusta was a good elder sister to you," she said. "She loved you and took care of you. If you do not love her you are the one to be ashamed. Never let me hear you say such a thing again as long as you live." If I was to love Augusta she couldn't have been bad, so I stopped thinking about it.

Augusta hacked knives. She washed dishes standing on a little stool, and father scolded her for letting the water run down her arms when she reached up, and for wasting soap making bubbles in the water; and for dawdling. After he had scolded her she would draw her eyebrows together and watch him out of the corner of her eyes; and if he wasn't looking she would hack the edges of the knives together. When we came from places, if she had stayed at home alone, father almost always punished her for something. Mother would take Teressa and me and go for a walk through the fields, and when we came back Augusta would be studying arithmetic, and crying.

If the knives were hacked, father would take them in their box out to the blacksmith shop. When I asked mother why, she said, "Hush!" so sharply I didn't ask again. Father would make Augusta go with him, and mother would not let me go along.

The day I was left entirely alone I went first to the pig corral. There was a tall corn crib beside it where I liked to climb. I would sit high above the pig, on top of the corn pile, and make fun of him when he squealed. He would stand below me, put his front feet on the top of the fence, and slant his nose up at me. I pretended the ears of corn started to roll under me—they did roll—and slid me down into the pen. I would pretend I ran for the fence, and the pig caught a piece of my dress just as I climbed over the bars. If I pretended hard enough I could make myself frightened; then I threw ears of corn down to the pig to make him stop looking at me. When father cleaned the cobs out of the corral he said he had been saving that corn for seed. He was annoyed about the pig's eating so much.

While I was sitting on the corn, after everything was still, I remembered about the knives. I thought about them, then I wondered about them. I wondered why Augusta hacked them, and why it was wrong. There was something dark and exciting about her doing it. The pig had gone to sleep. I climbed down from the corn crib and went to the house, through the kitchen into the pantry. The knife-box was on the lowest shelf, above my head, so I couldn't see into it without a chair. I took a chair from the kitchen, a wooden one not cane-seated, so my feet wouldn't break through it.

When I struck the blades together it made little pains run up and down my legs, as if it hurt the knives. Their edges caught, and made a rough feeling in my wrists when I pulled them apart. The first two knives were not fun. I laid one of them down and tried another, and another. I changed both knives, but they were all alike, none of them were any fun. I decided to wait until father and I were having a good time together some day, and promise not to do it but ask him why anyone hacked knives.

I put the knife-box away and went back to the pig. He was awake, and after I had fed him it was time for my own dinner. I set the table and ate; and cleared it and washed the dishes. When I dried my knife, the edge caught a thread on the tea towel and puckered it.

After dinner I didn't know what to do, so I scrubbed the kitchen. The floor wasn't dirty, but Teressa always scrubbed when she didn't have other things to do. I washed the first part of it hard, and the last not so hard. Each board was more worn in the middle than at the edges, so it was easiest to dry them lengthwise. I dried them crosswise, because the hardest way would be most right.

When father and mother and Teressa came home, they brought me a present, a bag of figs. I had never eaten figs before. After dinner mother acted queer, and put me to bed early, while she and father talked. They talked the next day, and kept sending me away from them. Teressa wanted to scold me for scrubbing the floor, but mother would not let her. She said the floor was a small matter, but Teressa said it would take three scrubbings to get it into shape again. It wasn't out of shape.

The third day father didn't go to plow. Mother sent Teressa outdoors, and called me in where she and father were. They asked me why I had hacked the knives. I had forgotten about doing it, because it hadn't been in my mind. It was as if I hadn't hacked them, since I hadn't found out why I shouldn't; and I answered quick that I didn't hack them.

Mother said, "You hacked the knives, and that was wrong; but it is a great deal worse not to tell the truth about it. You must tell why you did it."

I explained that I did try to hack them, but didn't know how. Father said, "You knew how all too well."

When I tried to explain about it, they asked me more and more questions. They asked me things that had not been in my mind before, whether Augusta had taught me to hack them, and if I had ever helped her do it. Father's face looked thin and white. He had never paid so much attention to anything I did, before, not even to making new poems. He said, "If I *knew* she did it to flout me, if I *knew* she did it in scorn of me, to fling back into my face the villainy of that infernal—"

Mother stopped him: "She did it because you suggested it by telling her not to. There is no mystery about it, except that you should have put such a thing into her head."

They asked me more questions, and talked about the rice. Mother asked if I didn't suppose she knew better how to cook rice than I, that I failed to do as she told me. I explained that I was afraid I had made a mistake in listening. They talked to me until I cried. I cried so hard that when I looked at their faces, their cheeks stretched out in wavery lines. If I half shut my eyes, lines of light came from their faces toward me. I was so interested in making the lines longer and shorter that I stopped crying, and they were discouraged with me.

Father went to the pantry and got the box of knives. He said, "For your punishment you must turn the grindstone while I smooth these out." I thought he was making a joke, because I always liked to turn the grindstone for him when he would let me. Usually he had Teressa help him; he said she was less erratic. I looked at him and laughed, but his eyes looked down at me, small and blue.

When my arms grew tired, the grindstone went slower and slower until it stopped. Father said, "Keep on turning." I explained about my arms, and he said, "Indeed?" He looked at me, whistling, and said, "Indeed?" again. "Find your sister and ask her to come here." But before I could start he called, "Dick!"

He said, "My son Richard, will you turn the grindstone for your father?" He called her *Richard* because she was Richard the Lion-Hearted.

Teressa said, "Yes . . . baby!" She meant me. She reached back with her heel, before she began turning, and stepped on my foot.

Father told me to go to the house and talk to mother. She asked me where the knives were. I said father was sharpening them. She asked why I wasn't turning the grindstone, and I told her Teressa was turning it because my arms were tired. She said I must learn that the way of the transgressor is hard, and that I should be ashamed to make Teressa undo my mischief. I knew a secret about Teressa, though I didn't tell it: *Teressa liked to do hard things to see whether she could or not.*

Mother asked me if I thought it was fair to make extra work for father, when he ought to be out plowing. I asked, "What work?" She said, "Sharpening the knives you hacked."

I sat without moving. When I understood things I had wondered about, it excited me inside.

I said, "It wasn't wrong to hack the knives." I meant it wasn't wrong in the way I had supposed. It was wrong in a way I knew, and not in a way I didn't know. There was nothing about doing it I had not found out.

Mother set me down hard on my feet. She put her hands on my shoulders and shook me until my head jerked back and forth. She said, "I can not understand your being so naughty." I couldn't either, so I didn't.

She said again that the way of the transgressor was hard, and told me to sit in a chair until she decided how to punish me. I picked out the hardest chair to sit in, not my little cane chair. She said I had been careful not to hack my own small white-handled knife that I ate with, and she would take it away from me; from now on I would have to eat with one of the others.

I said, "You can use if for a butter knife." I had heard her tell Teressa they would have to use my little knife for the butter, because Mrs. Clarington had borrowed the butter knife when she had company and not brought it back.

Sometimes I didn't know why mother was annoyed. She was annoyed now. She took my hand and said, "We will go to the bedroom. You must kneel down and tell God what you have done, and ask Him to forgive you and make you a good girl."

I didn't want to go to the bedroom. I wanted not to so much that my legs moved in different parts; I could notice my knees bend, and feel where my feet were. I had never prayed out loud, kneeling down, in the daytime. I prayed, usually, when I was swinging, because I liked to swing. I always thought of God as having a good disposition. It seemed unnecessary to bother him about the knives, since it was all finished, and I understood.

Mother made me come with her. She told me to pray. I didn't know how, so she prayed first to show me. While she prayed I was so uncomfortable that if it had been anyone but God I would have hated him. I almost did not like mother. I thought of something so naughty I didn't dare say it, even to myself. Usually when I was naughty it was an accident, but this time I was so tired of the knives I wanted to be bad. I whispered, "God said something to me."

Mother put her arms around me. "My little girl, my little, little girl," she said. I was afraid she wouldn't ask me "What?" She said, "What, dear?"

I said, "Silly."

It was a very uncomfortable morning. I sat in my high chair without speaking until dinner time. It was then I learned that the wide spaces on the clock between the figures were five minutes, not single minutes. I thought about people. I thought of them as if they were wrapped in layers of something thick like quilts, only not quilts, that kept them from knowing how things really were.

Late Fruit

Mother was planning to visit her sister. She had a reason for going that I didn't know. Her sister was my Aunt Esther. I did not understand, at first, that the two were the same, when father said, *to your sister.* When I found out it made me feel part comfortable and part disappointed. It was like sitting in my own chair instead of in one I had been told not to use.

Mother had known she was going for a long time before she went. The only thing she did not know was which of us she would take with her. There were three of us. There had been four until Augusta went to stay with her grandmother. Augusta and Carl had a grandmother, and Teressa and I had one. They lived in different places. Father and mother talked about who should go with her, when Teressa was feeding the chickens and Carl had gone to milk. If I did not look at them as they talked they did not send me away.

Deciding who was to go was like fitting the pieces of a puzzle together. They would fit only one way. Father and mother fitted the pieces around and around every way but the right one. I did not say this.

If mother took me with her it would leave Teressa alone with father and the hired men. Sometimes mother said, *alone with Carl.* I did not know why Teressa could not stay alone with Carl. They did not quarrel. Carl told Teressa things the hired men told him, that neither of them would tell me. Sometimes they played together, but not often, and would not let me play with them. They had a game called Being Enchanted. I shut my eyes and counted ten, and when I opened them they were not there.

If mother took both Teressa and me there would be no one left to cook for the men; and Teressa would have to leave school. She liked school. Mr. Kimmel was the first teacher who had been nice to her. Father didn't like him, because he taught grammar and said *I seen.* Father liked English and not grammar. Mother liked both. She knew grammar, and father did not. Mr. Kimmel lived by himself in a dugout close to the schoolhouse, and mother liked him because he whipped only boys bigger than himself. The teacher before him whipped only the little boys.

I didn't go to school. It was too far for me to walk. Teressa was angry because I studied algebra at home, so mother let her study physiology, and not me. Mother made me study algebra to punish me for a joke: I said, "Two peaches and two kittens are four." Mother looked at me to see whether I was being naughty or being stupid. I didn't look away from her, so she couldn't tell. She said, "Four what?" I said, "Four adds," quick, without laughing, so she couldn't tell again.

After that she taught me, "Two x and two x are four x; two y and two y are four y." I didn't say, "Two x and two y are four," because that didn't make me want to laugh.

It was interesting to learn arithmetic with x's. It was like not having to put a nightdress on. Mother forgot she was punishing me, and taught me pluses and minuses. I learned all my arithmetic out of the algebra. She wouldn't let me touch Teressa's Physiology, but I heard the lessons when Teressa recited them, unless she asked mother to send me away. When we were in bed I would whisper, "There are two hundred and eight bones in the human body," to see if Teressa was asleep. If she called mother, she wasn't.

Mother couldn't take me with her without Teressa, and she couldn't take us both. She had to have some one with her, coming back, to carry her satchel. She would have more to carry coming back. I wondered what Aunt Esther was going to send us. Father laughed when I asked, but mother shut her lips tight for me to stop talking. I wondered why she didn't take Carl. Carl was big. He was eleven. He was two years older than Teressa, and Teressa was three years older than I.

At dinner, when no one was talking about mother's visit, I asked why Carl didn't go. Father said Carl had to help milk. Father milked three cows, and Carl three. I said I would milk Carl's cows. Father's eyes twinkled, but mother said, "Don't be foolish."

I *wanted* to milk Carl's cows so he could go with mother. I had known how to milk for a long time. I learned on a cow that limped when she walked. She didn't stay with the other cows; father had turned her outside the fence, where she could get plenty to eat. The milk ran out of her bag, and I milked her for my kittens. She used to come where I was, to be milked; but after I could milk fast, she stopped giving much, and pawed dust over me when I tried to come near her.

The kittens had learned to have all the milk they wanted, and were hungry, so I had to milk other cows. The pan I used leaked, so it made me milk a good deal. The kittens were all fat. After they had eaten, their tails stuck straight out. The mother cats lapped the milk off the ground, and crowded in beside the kittens and ate, too, because they knew there was always more. I didn't mention milking to anyone.

I kept offering to do Carl's milking until mother was not pleased with me. She told father she ought to punish me, but didn't know how. I did not know what for. Father said that was a simple matter: give me a pail and tell me to come and milk; when I saw I couldn't, that would end it.

He called me early, the next morning, and told me if I was going to milk Carl's cows it was time to get up; I must show that I could, before Carl left.

I dressed fast. Usually I was slow, because there was a game I could play while I buttoned my shoes. Father took a pail, and gave me one. We carried them with our outside arms, so I could take his hand on the way to the corral. It was not bright outdoors yet, everything was one color. Father put my pail under Old Whitey (she knew me), and gave me his milking stool. He went to the other side of the corral to milk Young Whitey. Old Whitey had big teats and was easy to milk. Young Whitey milked hard, and kicked. I used to chase her away, before I milked in the afternoons, so when she saw me in the corral it made her keep stepping farther away to look at me. It took father a long time to get her milked. He said she was possessed of the devil. I finished Old Whitey before he was through, and he said, "All right, all right," when I called to him; "I'll be there in a moment." When he saw the milk in my pail he said "Ju-pi-ter Pluvius!"

He took our pails to the house before we milked the other cows. He said, "She can milk."

The next night father asked, "Why *not* take Carl with you? It might do the blockhead good. He might even learn to close his mouth." Carl used to hold his mouth open, and father said, "Carl, close your mouth," every time he looked at him. Mother thought Carl couldn't breathe well, but father said he kept his mouth open out of inherent perversity, to annoy him. We had a mule that let his lower lip hang down, and kept its tongue between its teeth. Father hit it under the chin, every time he came near it, to make it bite its tongue. The mule learned to pull its tongue in, and stretch its head high out of reach to one side, away from father. It made father laugh. He said that since he had succeeded in making an impression on the mule, he had begun to have hopes of influencing Carl.

Mother took Carl with her. Before she left, there was a lot of getting ready to do. Father told Carl, every morning, to count the number of persons he saw on the train who went around with their mouths hanging open, and notice the look of intelligence it gave them. Mother told Teressa how to do everything, and made father promise that she should not miss a day of school. Father promised. She told me how to set the table at noon, and to put on bread and butter without telling, and whatever else Teressa cooked in the morning before she went to school.

I set the table the first day. Father got up twice, while we were eating, once to get the sugar, and once to get the butter. We didn't talk, but we looked at each other and laughed. The second day father told Teressa it was too hard for her to go to school while mother was gone. He called her his son Dick, Richard the Lion-Hearted, and said she could stay out of school until mother came back. I do not remember about meals after that. Teressa got them. At first she cried all day after father had gone from the house. I milked three cows in the morning, and three at night, and the rest of the time I played.

Except for milking, and seeing *Lost in London*, only one thing made mother's being away different from her being at home. That was father's eating her peaches.

When mother left, the peaches were not ripe. Before she came back they were all gone. They grew ripe and fell to the ground. Teressa canned them all day, and cried. Mother didn't know they were being canned, because she thought Teressa was in school. Mother liked peaches. Every time she wrote me a letter, she put in it, "Save me some peaches." The wind got cold, and the leaves fell off the peach trees. One day when I was playing in the farthest orchard, I found a tree that still had fruit on it. The leaves were so nearly gone that I could see the peaches on a high branch. Some lay under the tree. They were smooth, white-skinned peaches, pink on one side. They felt cold to my hands, and were mealy and not very sweet. I picked all I could find, and carried them to the house in my apron. I put them on the high kitchen shelf where the clock was. Every day I looked at the tree. Some of the peaches I could reach with a stick, and I gathered all I cold make fall. One day I got four. There were eleven on the shelf, altogether.

When father wound the clock before Sunday, he saw the peaches. He said, "Hello!" and took one. He ate it. I watched his teeth sink into it. I felt heavy inside, not like crying, and not like speaking. He took another. I told him they were mother's. I told him over and over. He ate six. He said they were a poor variety, quite dry and insipid.

When he started to reach for them the next night, I told him again I was saving them for mother. I pulled at his arm until he looked at me. He laughed without making any sound, as he sometimes did with Teressa and mother. He said, "Your mother does not need peaches. She has not done her duty." I watched him to see what he meant. Everything except the lamp was still and dark. He stopped looking at me, and said mother had had an abundance of fruit where she was, and would not care for peaches; and that a high, warm shelf was a poor place to keep them. Only one was left.

The next morning there were two peaches under the tree, and these were the last. There was not one more. The branches were bare, and I could see. I put the two new peaches and the warm one together in the writing desk, but father asked for them, that night. I had written mother that there were eleven, and would be more. She asked in every letter how many there were now. I didn't answer.

When mother came home there were things that kept her from asking for the peaches right away. One was that we had gone to the theater the

night before she came. We drove eighteen miles to see *Enoch Arden*, and
when we got to the theater the play was *Lost in London*. I had never been
in a theater before, but it seemed as if I had. I liked everything about it,
but I was the only one of us who had a good time. Being where people
were made Teressa's head ache, and father was disappointed because
we weren't seeing *Enoch Arden*. He had seen that play with his wife,
once, and wanted to see it again. He said, *with my wife*, and I said, *with
mother*, because I knew they were the same. Teressa hurt me with her
elbow and said "Little idiot!" under her breath. After the theater we
waited for the train that mother and Carl might come on. They didn't
come. We drove home in the moonlight. Teressa slept, but father and I
made rhymes. The last one came right in front of the house:

Three o'clock
At the hitching block!

Father drove back alone the next day to meet mother and Carl.
He said we need not mention having gone to the theater. But he told
mother, and that made it seem queer that we hadn't.

The first afternoon that mother and I were alone after she came back,
she sat in the rocking-chair by the kitchen window to talk to me. She
asked me if I thought it was right to got to the theater and not tell her
about it. I said, "Father took us," so she asked if I had been lonesome for
her while she was away. I said, "No." Then she said, "You may bring me
my peaches now. I feel as though I could eat one." Her voice sounded
as if she were punishing me.

It was so hard to answer about the peaches that before I spoke she
said, "You couldn't resist temptation, could you? I knew you would eat
them before I got back."

My dress was loose. I could feel my body shake inside it. After a
while mother put her arm around me, and felt it, too. She took me on
her lap.

It was hard to explain about the peaches, because I didn't understand
about them. Something had happened while mother was away that she
and father were not happy about, and eating the peaches seemed part of
it. I hoped mother would tell me it was wrong for father to eat them. It
seemed wrong. If it was wrong, and he did it, I would understand and

not care. I did not know whether things grown people did were ever not right. Mother did not tell me. She said all the orchard was father's, but I explained to her why those peaches were mine. She said, "It was the love, not the peaches—surely you did not think it was for the peaches that I cared." I did not understand. She said, "Since you thought of me, and denied yourself, it is as if I had had the fruit."

She held me on her lap and rocked me until it was time to get supper. I lay and looked at her face. Here eyes were closed. It was the first time I had noticed that tears could come from under a person's lids when they were shut.

Wild Plums

I knew about wild plums twice before I tasted any.

The first time was when the Sunday-school women were going plumming. Father hunched his shoulders and laughed without making any sound. He said wild plums were small and inferior, and told us of fruits he had eaten in Italy.

Mother and father were surprised that Mrs. Guare and the school-teacher would go with Mrs. Slump to gather plums. I knew it was not nice to go plumming, but didn't know why. I wanted to go, once, so I would understand. The women had stopped at the house to invite mother. She explained that we did not care for wild plums; but father said we feared to taste the sacred seed lest we be constrained to dwell forever in the nether regions.

Mrs. Slump said, "Huh? You don't eat the pits. You spit 'em out," and father hunched his shoulders and laughed the noiseless laugh that bothered mother.

When father talked to people he didn't like he sorted his words, and used only the smooth, best ones. Mother explained to me that he had spoken only German when he was little.

After the women had gone, mother and father quarreled. They spoke low so I would not hear them. Just before mother sent me out to play she said that even wild plums might give savor to the dry bread of monotony.

The second time I knew about plums was at Mrs. Slump's house when she was making plum butter. She said she couldn't ask us in, because the floor was dirty from stirring jam. The Slumps didn't use chairs. They had boxes to sit on, and the children sat on the floor with the dogs. They were the only family I was acquainted with that had hounds. I wanted to go in. We had never visited them. We were at their house this time because father needed to take home a plow they had borrowed. Father did not like to have his machinery stand outdoors. He had a shed where he kept plows when he was not using them, but the Slumps left theirs where they unhitched.

Mrs. Slump was standing in the door with her back toward us when we drove up. She was fat, and wore wrappers. Her wrapper was torn down the back.

Mr. Slump came out, and father talked to him. He was tall and lean. Mrs. Slump came, too, and leaned on the buggy wheel. Mother and father sat on the front seat of the buggy, and Teressa and I on the back seat. Teressa was older than I, and had longer legs. When she stretched her feet straight out she could touch the front seat with her toes, and I couldn't. She bumped the seat behind mother, and mother turned around and told her to stop. My feet didn't touch father's seat, so I wasn't doing anything and didn't have to stop it. Teressa pinched me.

I climbed out of the buggy without asking if I might. Teressa started to tell mother, but waited to see if I was going to do something interesting. I was going to walk around behind Mrs. Slump. She had no stockings on, and the Sunday-school women had said she didn't wear underclothes. I wanted to see if this was so.

Mother called me back. Sometimes mother knew what I intended to do without asking me. She took hold of my arm, hard, as I climbed onto the buggy step, and said under her breath, "I'd be ashamed!" Her face twisted, because she tried not to stop smiling at Mrs. Slump while she shook my arm. I kept trying to explain, but she wouldn't let me. I was not going to say what she thought I was.

Mr. Slump said he would bring the plow back in the morning. Father wanted to take it home himself, then; but Mr. Slump said he wouldn't hear to it, being as how he had borrowed it, and all. He would hook it behind the lumber wagon next day, and leave it in the road. They were going after more plums, and would be passing the house anyway.

The next morning after breakfast, father, mother, and I were in the kitchen. Teressa had scraped the plates and gone to feed the chickens. She did not like to sit still while people talked. She liked to do things that made her move around. Mother and father were talking, and I was looking out of the window. If I looked at the sun, and then looked away, it made enormous morning-glories float over the yard. Father had told me they were in my eyes and not in the air, so I didn't call him to look at them any more. While I was watching them, Clubby Slump came up the lane in the middle of a lavender one. Clubby was bigger than I, and stupider. When anyone spoke to him he stood with his mouth open and didn't answer. His hair needed combing, and he didn't use a handkerchief. Mother said good morning to him. He pointed to a wagon at the end of the lane, said, "Plums," and ran back down the path.

Father and mother started toward the road, and I went ahead of them. The wagon had stopped at the foot of the cottonwood lane. Mr. Slump sat on the high board seat, holding the reins. Mrs. Slump was beside him, with the baby on her lap. Liney Slump was between them. On the seat behind were Mrs. Guare and two women I didn't know. The rest of the wagon was full of children. Mr. Slump had forgotten the plow.

"All you-uns pile in," Mrs. Slump called to us. "We're goin' plummin' on the Niniscaw an' stay all night. There ain't no work drivin' you this time a' year no way, so jus' pile in. We got beddin' for everybody."

Mr. Slump was not looking at us. He sat looking ahead at the horses, and saying, "I *tole* you they-all wouldn't go, but you *would* stop." Mrs. Slump answered him without turning her head, "There now, paw, you hush," and went on talking to us.

I had not supposed one could live so long without breathing as I lived while I waited for us to answer. My heartbeats shook my collar—a lace collar that accidentally hung by one end down my chest, instead of being around my neck.

I waited for mother to lift her foot and plant it on the wagon hub, ready for "pilin' in"; for father to take her elbow, and lift. Everyone would laugh a little, and talk loud. They always did when women got into wagons. I had never seen mother climb into a wagon, but I knew how it would be. I wondered if father would jump in without remembering to toss me up first. Father got into wagons quick, without laughing or joking. If they both forgot me, the children would see me, and could lean over the endboard and dangle me up by one arm. I thought frantically of Teressa.

Then father was speaking, and my breath came back.

He was saying, "If you happen on a plum thicket, an outcome I think highly improbable, you still face the uncertainty of finding fruit. The season has been too dry. And should you find plums, they will prove small and acrid and unfit for human consumption."

My collar hung limp and motionless. My heart was dead. Father was spoiling things again.

Mrs. Slump said, "They make fine jell," and Mr. Slump began once more, "I *tole* you they-all wouldn't come—" He was gathering up the lines.

I dreaded to see mother's face, feeling the ended look it would have; but I knew I must smile at her not to care. Strangely enough, she had a polite look on her face. It was the look that made my fingers think of glass. My mind slipped from it without knowing what it meant. Mother was smiling.

"Really, it isn't possible for us to go with you to-day," she said. "It was kind of you to ask us. I hope you will have a lovely outing, and find plenty of fruit."

As she spoke she glanced at me. She stepped closer, and took my hand. Mrs. Slump looked down at me, too, and asked, "Can't the kid go? Kids like bein' out."

Mother's hand closed firmly on mine. "I'm afraid not, without me. Besides," with a severe look at my collar, "she is not properly dressed."

"Oh, we kin wait while she takes off that purty dress," Mrs. Slump urged; but mother flushed, and shook her head. Mr. Slump was twitching at the lines, and clucking to the horses. His last "I *tole* you" was lost in shouted good-bys, and the wagon clattered down the road.

Mother walked back to the house still holding my hand. Inside the kitchen, she turned to me. "Would you really have gone with those—" she hesitated, "with those persons?"

"They were going to sleep outdoors all night," I said.

Mother shuddered. "Would you have gone with them?"

"Mrs. Guare was with them," I parried, knowing all she did not voice.

"Would you have gone?"

"Yes."

She stood for a long time at the window, looking out at the prairie horizon, then searched my face curiously. "It might have been as well," she said; "It might be as well," and turning, she began to clear the breakfast table.

The next day I played in the road. Usually I spent the afternoons under the box elder trees, or by the ditch behind the machine sheds, where dragon flies and pale blue moths circled just out of reach. This day I spent beside the road. Mother called me to the house to fill the cob-box, and called me again to gather eggs in the middle of the afternoon. She called me a third time. Her face looked uncomfortable.

She said, "If the Slumps go by, do not ask them for plums."

Mother knew I would not ask.

"If they offer you any, do not take them."

"What shall I say?"

"Say you do not care for them."

"If they make me take them?"

"Refuse them."

When the Slumps came in sight the horses were walking. The Niniscaw was fifteen miles away, and the team was tired. I thought I could talk to the children as the wagon went by, but just before it reached me Mr. Slump hit the horses twice with a willow branch. They trotted, and the wagon rattled past.

The children on the last seat were riding backward, facing me. They laughed, and waved their arms. Clubby reached behind him, and caught up a handful of plums. The wagon bed must have been half full. He flung the plums toward me, and then another handful. They fell, scattering, in the thick dust which curled around them in little eddies, almost hiding them before I could catch them up.

The plums were small and red, and warm to my fingers. I brushed them on the front of my dress, and dropped them in my up-gathered apron. I waited only for one secret rite before I ran, heart pounding, to tell my mother what I had discovered.

She interrupted me. "Did they see you picking them up?"

I thought of myself standing like Clubby Slump, mouth open, without moving. I laughed till two plums rolled out of my apron. "Oh, yes! I had them picked up almost before the dust stopped wiggling. I called, 'Thank you.'"

Still mother was not pleased.

"Throw them away," she said. "Surely you would not wish to eat something flung to you in the road."

It was hard to speak. I moved close to her and whispered, "Can't I keep them?"

Mother left the room. It seemed long before she came back. She put her arm around me, and said, "Take the plums to the pump and wash them thoroughly. Eat them slowly, and do not swallow the skins. You will not want many of them, for you will find them bitter and not fit to eat."

I went without speaking, knowing I would never tell her they were sweet on my tongue as wild honey, holding the warmth of sand that sun had fingered, and the mystery of water under leaning boughs.

For I had eaten one at the road.

The Flyleaf in the Book of Disillusion

We had trees.

We had orchards, but we had trees besides.

Everyone had orchards—peach and cherry trees, and sometimes long plum rows. Plums were vaguely undesirable. We didn't have any. We were the norm. Grape arbors were wonderful, like things in books. We had none, but we would have, some day.

Father sneered at people who had things we didn't. Mother never sneered. She loved people in spite of herself as soon as she was sorry for them, and she was sorry for them as soon as they began to talk to her. But even mother's tone was delicately final when she said, "We do not care for . . ."

Yes, plums were déclassé, especially wild plums.

We had trees. Cottonwoods. And osage oranges—not hedges such as shiftless people used instead of barbed wire fences, but single trees pruned high, with big trunks. There were five box elders: three men and one woman tree, who were always unfamiliar, like persons one passed in town without speaking; and one big father box elder in whose branches I spent long hours. Two Ailanthus trees stood outside the pantry window. These were not like real trees. They belonged to the dark strange things that meant something other than themselves. They were father's trees. Mother, who loved always, hated them. She never looked at them, never spoke of them, yet I knew she hated them. I wondered if they were part negro.

The cottonwoods stood on the north side of the lane running west from the road to the house. There were red cottonwoods and yellow cottonwoods. They were tall. They were the tallest things in the world. They were taller than the windmill, which was over a thousand feet. I knew about the windmill. I had asked father—he was planing red cedar posts for the windmill's legs—if thirty feet was more than a thousand. He chuckled and said, "Yes. Thirty feet more. One is a fact and the other is an exaggeration." What he said made little shadows of what he meant on my mind, and we both laughed. The cottonwoods were so tall they hardly noticed the windmill after it was once built.

Early in the spring, early, before I had begun to ask, "How long is it until my birthday?" and my mother to answer, "Three months, now," the cottonwoods would begin to look important. They would sway a little and glance at each other, or stand very still and wait. They were not uneasy. They were not uneasy, because they were old and understood everything; but they were waiting, and their highest tips were beginning to swell.

Then came days when the hens' summons was indolent and compelling, days when they sauntered around talking to themselves, or threw showers of rich earth as they ruffled into the side of a sunny bank. Men were plowing, and I was never in the house. Mother's admonition, "Don't go out without your sunbonnet," just missed me around the corner of the building. Suddenly summer was droning everywhere, and the cottonwoods were wattled in red and yellow.

The catkins hung on the highest branches, festooned and lovely, mysterious colored lace against the sky. The nearest branches of the trees were inaccessible; above my head—above my brother's head—so the lane cottonwoods were never climbed. On these lower branches, also, catkins hung. They were coarser and indefinably different from those above. Besides, they fell off and lay thick on the ground, and were quite rough and ugly with knobby green lumps near the stem. We walked on them under the trees, and even made a game of stepping on them. I was ashamed, afterward, and picked up the bruised catkins to bury them in shallow graves, and tried to make my feet stop thinking about them.

In the topmost branches hung the delicate panicles for which I ached. I could not tell which was harder to bear, to see them swing gently in the soft wind, as if they were standing tiptoe to look beyond the horizon, or to watch them hang motionless, meaning something I could not understand. Motionless, they frightened me; so that I ran away and hid in the hayloft, or flung myself against the stubborn trunks in a vain attempt to make the branches stir. Dancing, they excited me beyond reason.

One day, a thousand years long, when the sunshine ran its fingers over my face if I closed my eyes, our parents had gone to town. We three children had been left behind, with the usual injuctions to do this and do that, and refrain from the other. In the afternoon we were together in the yard. We were almost never out of doors together. Teressa usually stayed in the house and peeled potatoes, or stood on a chair so she could reach to wash dishes; and Carl ran after the hired men. When Carl and Teressa did play, they were Enchanted. They stayed right by my side where they had been, but they couldn't speak and couldn't be seen. They had played this game all the morning. It bothered me a little, and made me feel queer, because I was afraid they were looking at what I was thinking. I watched things outside me and tried not to think. They had grown tired of being enchanted, and had come into sight from behind me. Carl discovered that I wanted a cottonwood blossom. I pointed out the very one. Teressa reminded him that we were forbidden to climb trees when our parents were away. Carl remembered that the last thing mother had said was for them to take good care of Veve, and how could they take good care of her, he argued, unless they got her a cottonwood blossom when she wanted it?

Teressa was sufficiently reassured to brace her stocky shoulders against the tallest tree, and help Carl climb until he could clutch the lowest branch. After that her advice alternated between telling him he was a fool for risking his neck to humor a baby, and encouraging him if he showed signs of turning back.

He climbed. He climbed. He passed the broad crotches and the diminishing upper branches. At last he stood in the highest notch he dared attempt, and stretched out his hand.

I looked away while he picked the catkin.

Teressa and he were standing in front of me, pressing into my palms the fairy tassels. At first I thought they were playing a joke on me, but in an instant I knew! I knew, irrevocably, and burst into tears, silent flooding tears that came easily and left my spirit clean. The two plied me with questions. Wasn't it the blossom I wanted? Did I want more? Did I want a yellow one? Did I want red ones? All I could do was to shake my head, *no, no,* and whisper, "Go away!"

Teressa stamped her foot and appealed to space to know if I were not a most "pervoking child." (I was secretly grateful to her that she seldom took tears seriously.) Carl was troubled. He did not know me well. Finally Teressa declared, "We'll ask her just once more what's the matter, and if she won't tell we'll run away and hide!"

She leaned over me and shook my arm, demanding, "What are you crying for?"

Humor broke through my tears. I could taste their salty trickle at the corners of my smile as I proffered that ultimate outrage: "I was crying for fun."

"Then let's run away from her," snorted my sister, and two pairs of legs, swifter than mine, were around the house and out of sight.

But I knew why I had cried, though words to tell it were not yet mine. I had opened the great book of disillusion, and from the flyleaf deduced the entire volume. I knew, once and for all, that fairy things against the sky fall humdrum, to be trampled under foot.

Trees of Heaven

Father never rested on the porch in the evening, where the others sat. If he came outdoors after the chores were done, when supper was over, he went farther down the walk where he could look at the Ailanthus trees. Father called them Ailanthus trees, and mother, Ailantus. I called them Ailanthus.

There were two of them. They stood outside the west pantry window. The pantry was long, and had a kitchen table in it where mother rolled cookies. It had a sink with two pumps, one from the well and one from the cistern; and a trough with cold water in it, where mother set crocks of milk. Mother did most of her work in the pantry, so she saw the Ailanthus trees all day. They were the only trees in the yard that she did not like. She said they should have been planted some place where she would not have to look at them.

The pantry sink drained into a pool beside the trees. The water was supposed to run off along the gooseberry bushes, but it didn't; so there was a hollow where the water always stood. Mother did not let us play there. That was why I was not well acquainted with the Ailanthus trees. I had never taken hold of them. Their trunks were small, and I wondered whether I could reach around one with both hands. The bark looked smooth and gray, but I didn't know how it felt.

The trees were strangers. They were like foreigners. Both were tall and thin, with branches only at the top. One was crooked. Their leaves were dark, not like other tree-leaves. They were fancier, and had red on them. I thought of Ailanthus trees and castor beans together. They

made me feel the same way, except that castor beans were not nice. Mrs.
Clarington had castor beans, and father did not like her.

The wind broke a tip from the taller tree, and blew it along the path.
I took it to mother. She said, "Take the thing outside." When I looked
at her to see why, she said she did not like the odor. The blossoms did
smell queer.

Father liked to look at the Ailanthus trees against the sunset. He held
my hand while we walked around the yard and talked about them. He
said they were exotic, and quite palm-like in aspect. I said his words over
and over in my mind. He showed me why they were like palm trees—
because they had leaflets up and down a broad stem. The Ailanthus was
an East Indian tree, father said, and the Indians called it the Tree of
Heaven.

One of the trees worried father. He walked around and around it,
looking up into its branches. The next spring it was dead. Father said
he would uproot both trees. Mother thought it silly to destroy two lives
because one happened to die, but father said that when one died, it was
kinder to consign both to oblivion.

The day father took out the Ailanthus trees he did no other work.
He brought tools from the shed besides an ax—a grub hoe and a spade.
I waited to watch him cut the first tree down, so I could see the top and
gather some leaves to press; but father told me to play on the other side
of the house. The pantry window was open, and mother called me. She
put me in the front room to sew. I sewed two squares of cloth together
to make a quilt. When I was ready to play she unlocked the front door
and told me to go down the front path to the orchard, and when I came
back to come up the path, and in at the front door. When mother told
us exactly how to do things we did them that way.

The next time I saw the place where the Ailanthus trees had been,
they were gone. The ground was smooth, covered with sand and little
stones left from making cement for the cellar walls. It looked quiet and
neat. The trees were not on the ground, and they were not cut up for
firewood in the kitchen wood-box. I saw scratches on the ground where
they had been dragged away. I put my feet on the marks until I came
to the blacksmith shop.

The trees were not behind the shed, nor in the ditch beyond. After a time I knew father had burned them in the forge where he heated plowshares.

I asked mother why father took away both Ailanthus trees, and she told me not to question her. I asked father, and he said, "It lies beyond your comprehension, my child." I asked Teressa, when she was holding me on her lap. Her lap was not very big, and it was easy to slide off. She said, "Father and *somebody* planted an Ailanthus tree on each side of the gate." She made a song of it under her breath while she rocked me, "Father and *somebody*, father and *somebody*."

I wondered about the gate. We had no gates except at the corral, and horses would trample trees there. When I asked Teressa about it she said, "Little idiot! Not *this* house. Not *this* gate." Then she pushed me off her lap and said she would tell mother I was asking questions about things that did not concern me.

It bothered me to know part of a thing, and not why it was so. It kept me from wanting to play with my dolls. After I had asked Teressa about the trees there was no one else to ask. I went into the yard to look at the place where they had been. It was dusk. I could imagine the trees against the sky, but they were flatter and darker than when they had been alive, and I could not make their leaves stir in my mind.

Plaster of Paris

I climbed up on the chair in front of father's desk. If I pulled at the desk it might fall over on me, so I didn't. I wanted to look at the statue standing above the cubby-holes where father kept letters. The statue was one of the things that were father's and not mother's, like the Ailanthus trees and the cameos with gold fringe that mother did not wear, and the two ivory paper knives. Mother's things were the black-cherry tree and the *Advocate and Guardian* and her pearl-handled pen.

I had never looked at the statue before, because it was ugly. Mother thought it was ugly, I knew, though she had never told me she thought so. I looked at it this time because I wanted to pretend the brown marble at the bottom was chocolate candy, and think how it would taste. I had never tasted chocolate creams, but I had tasted sweet chocolate once.

The statue had seemed only dark and brown, but when I saw it close it had a beautiful red color under the surface, with strange markings. The lowest part of the statue, nearest my eyes, was square. I could think of slicing a thin narrow strip from it, and eating it. Above the square part was a gold band, and above that the marble was round. It was this marble that I looked at longest. I tried to say to myself what the markings looked like. Some were like cobwebs, and some were like crinkled lightning in the sky at night. One was twisted like grapevine stems in an arbor. Father had showed me an arbor, once, when we were driving home from town. On one side of the marble were marks that made me think of a mountain where giants had fought and fallen down, though I didn't know why. That part went out of sight on the other side, so I couldn't see how it finished.

After I had looked at the marble I looked at the rest of the statue. I hadn't meant to look at it. What I saw was flowers—tiny daisies and roses, tinier than star grass, mixed with leaves; and another flower I didn't know.

It was because I looked to see where the flowers came from that I saw they were around a man's and woman's shoulders. The two were kissing. The flower chain was around them both, and fell across her neck. The petals had lovely gold and brown lights in them. A daisy lay against the woman's flesh, and I saw how soft her breast was, and her arm. I could feel them over my face and body, like a person's. I looked at the statue a long time, almost frightened.

When I got down from the chair I was careful not to rock the desk. I went to the kitchen to tell mother what I had found out. She was standing at the table making something with dough. Teressa was sitting in my little rocking-chair peeling potatoes for supper. She was older than I, and helped mother. I stood close by mother, watching the dough. I said, "The statue is beautiful."

Mother stood still, not moving her hands. She said, "It is hideous. Go outdoors."

I went out softly, and around to the front door. I climbed up to look at the statue again. This time I looked at the man and woman first.

The woman's hair had gold in it, like the daisies. The man's had, too, but I noticed the woman's hair most. It was tied back and heaped on her head, and fell around her shoulder and neck. I could feel the man's arm being around her, even where it didn't show. The stillness about the statue made tears in my eyes.

I was so sure mother would want to understand about its being pretty that I went outside and into the kitchen again, to wait until she didn't look busy. I said, "The flowers are pretty."

Mother asked, "What flowers, dear?"

"The flowers around their necks."

Mother's face made me think of something crumpled up and straightened out again. She said, "Yes, they are beautiful. Now run outdoors and play."

After that I looked at the statue whenever I thought about it. At first I looked only when I was alone; but once I forgot, and climbed up on the chair when father and mother were both sitting in the room. Father was reading the New York *Sun* and mother was reading the Bible. Father looked up and saw me, and said, "Already the child has a fine perception of beauty."

Mother and father quarreled because he said that. Mother did not like to have father say things before us that would make us be conceited. After mother went from the room father took the statue down and showed it to me. He had me hold it to see how heavy it was. He told me it was rosewood marble. The square part was the base. The round marble was the pedestal. The flower I didn't know was a narcissus. The leaves were ivy. Father told me I could dust the statue every day. He found a fine, soft brush that took all the dust out of the creases in the daisy petals. Mother did not like to have me dust it, so I tried harder to do it right.

It was because I knew about Tennyson that I learned something more about the statue. Tennyson's poems belonged to father, too. He had two Tennysons and let me read the oldest one. I knew all of *Lady Clare* and *Lord of Burleigh*, and most of the *Vision of Sin*, beginning with the wrinkled ostler, in the part where the lines were short, and rhymed.

When I read I lay on my stomach. If I put my elbows on the leaves it kept the wind from blowing them, but it made them come out at the back, too; so all the pages I liked best were loose. Mother and father talked about my reading the *Vision of Sin*. They talked about whether I understood it. Father said he didn't fully grasp the conception of "the awful rose of dawn," and was going to ask me what I understood by it. Mother said it was silly to ask a child such questions. I sat on the porch with my hands between my knees and laughed, only not out loud, because the part they were talking about was the part I didn't read.

In Memoriam was in Tennyson, but it wasn't good to read. One day when I was dusting the statue I noticed writing on the gold band around the pedestal. It said: *In Memoriam—Lovers long betrothed were they*. I knew it was a mistake, because that line came in *Lady Clare*. Then I was bothered over having thought it was wrong, because the words might be in both poems. I looked at all the lines of *In Memoriam*. Those were not there.

I thought and thought about the line, trying to see how it could be right. I did not like to ask father, because he cared so much for the statue he would feel sorry if it was wrong. I would have told mother, but when I showed her mistakes it was always I who was wrong and not the book. I found out about *In Memoriam*. It meant being dead.

I asked mother if the people in the statue were dead. She looked as if I had frightened her, and wanted to know why I asked. I didn't tell.

Father and mother talked about the statue again. They talked that night, and the next day. I was uncomfortable. Father said, "I will destroy the thing." I said, "Let me have it. I will keep it with my things." They looked at me as if I were some place else.

Father said he would obliterate the inscription.

Mother said, "Can you obliterate it from my soul?"

Father took the statue to the blacksmith shop, but came back to ask if I might help him a bit. Mother said, "No."

I carried my doll to the porch bedroom, and went around the side of the house to the shop where father was. He showed me what was the trouble. The gold band lay so close to the marble he was afraid the file might mar the edges of the stone. He was going to take the statue apart before he filed the letters off. The statue was not all in one piece. It was put together on a rod. The rod went through the marble base and pedestal, and held up the bronze part. Underneath the base was a hollow place for a nut on the end of the rod. When father started to pull the rod out, he found it had plaster of paris around it. He wanted me to hold the statue while he chipped at the plaster with a chisel. He was afraid to put it in the vise for fear he would blemish it. We worked on it a long time. My arms ached. It was growing dark in the shed. Father put the statue in the vise and wrenched the rod loose. It bent, coming out. He filed the letters off.

While he put the statue together again, he talked to me. Whatever the statue had been to him, he said, to me he wanted it to be only beauty. He had never wished to make it mean anything else to me. It was the work of a great artist. He showed me the letters HOUDON cut in the marble. I had not seen them when I dusted, because they were where they didn't show much.

Father said, "I honor my wife with all the love and fealty one can bear the dead."

I broke what he said apart in my mind as we walked toward the house. His wife . . . that was mother. The dead . . . *In Memoriam* . . . that was the statue. Perhaps the reason she didn't like the statue was because she didn't know this.

There was poetry that I had know always, because father repeated it to me before I could remember. Sometimes I said it back to him when we were together. We were thinking about statues, so I said, "A tale of fairy ships, with a swan's wing for a sail!"

Father made a noise as if he hurt. I asked him what was the matter. He said, "The pain, the pain!"

Usually when father hurt himself he swore a little. Mother would say, "*Please*, Henry, not before the children!" and I would be polite like the Sunday-school women and say, "Oh, never mind about me."

The statue wasn't quite true on its pedestal after father changed it, because the rod was bent. The place where the letters had been filed off was flat, and of different color from the rest. I loved the statue less. I knew how it was made, and felt sorry for it. When I dusted it I was ashamed without knowing what I had done. After a time I stopped looking at it, and it was Teressa who tended it when she dusted other things.

The Truth

A grotesque absurdity," said my father.

"It is better than nothing," said mother.

"It is infinitely worse than nothing," said father.

Mother did not answer. She was stitching a seam on the sewing machine, and couldn't look up. The machine was old; so she had to watch the thread.

"It is a travesty," said father. "The entire conception is a travesty on truth, but this is a travesty on the poesy that lies back of the conception."

Mother answered, and with spirit, this time: "It has the truth of kindliness and good will, and wanting to give happiness, and making the best of hardships."

They were talking about the Christmas tree at the schoolhouse, which the Sunday-school women were arranging for the children. Mrs. Guare and Mrs. Slump had come to tell mother about it, one day when father was in town. They came in the morning. No one visited us very often. Mrs. Guare had a pleasant voice, and her words were like mother's. Mrs. Slump made me listen harder, because she used words I didn't know. She didn't wear stockings under her shoes in summer time; and Mrs. Crachy said she didn't wear underclothes under her wrapper. I could have found out, once, but mother wouldn't let me.

After the women had talked for a time I stopped listening to them. I was playing that my doll was delirious and had to be held in bed. When she slept I read the New York *Sun*. I read the *Cream of the Telegraph*, because the stories were short and had space between them. The words were short, too, and I knew what they meant.

I knew about the *Sun*. Father had told me. His father learned to read English out of it when he first came to this country. Father knew Dana. I wasn't sure in my mind who was Dana and who was Goethes Faust. Father talked about them both. When father talked about them I felt inside the same way I did when mother told me about God. Father was ashamed of me because I thought Goethes Faust was one man. He said, "Preposterous absurdity!" and told me Goethe wrote Faust, but didn't tell me what he wrote him. I did not quite understand about Goethe and Faust; but I didn't entirely understand about God, either.

I stopped reading and put the paper under me—I was sitting on the floor—because Mrs. Slump said, "Lookiter pertend to read!"

The women and mother were bothered about something, so I watched them. Mrs. Slump said: "I ain't no hand to go beaten around the bush. It's just thisaway. We-all like you, and want you in our Crismus tree; but if you're scairt to ask your man for the money, being as how he's an onbeliever, we want you in anyhow, whether you given nothin' or not."

When mother laughed she sounded like flowers. She laughed now. She wasn't bothered any more. She said, "Of course I want to help with the Christmas tree. What my husband believes doesn't matter—does it?" She smiled at them. "Put my name down for whatever the rest are giving."

She rose and went into the living room—we were sitting in the kitchen where there was a fire—and beyond, into her bedroom. She came back with her pocketbook.

"How much did you put me down for?" mother asked. Mrs. Guare had a list of names in her hand.

"A quarter," said Mrs. Guare, "that's what the rest of us gave."

Mother handed her a coin. "Will that be enough?" she asked.

"Yes. We thought it would seem friendly if we all gave the same."

Mrs. Slump stared openly at mother. "Can you give it right out, thataway, without seein' the mister first?" she asked.

Mother laughed again, "Oh, yes!"

The women began to talk faster, planning the Christmas program.

There was to be candy in colored sacks. They would have a Santa Claus. Claud Slump would be Santa Claus. Mrs. Slump looked in my direction, and said very loud, "Claud can go out and get Santy when we are ready for him." Mother smiled at me and said, "She will not tell."

"She knows about Santa Claus?" asked Mrs. Guare.

Mother said *yes*, again. I was surprised that anyone would think I had not heard of Santa Claus. I had seen pictures of him. I didn't know, until mother told me, that some children thought he was real besides his clothes.

The candy bags were to be made of pink and white mosquito netting. Mrs. Guare thought Santa could come in carrying the sacks in a clothes basket.

"Oh, hang them on the tree," mother cried, "they will help fill it up. We'll string popcorn and cranberries, and festoon it all over!" Mother's cheeks were red and her eyes shone.

"There ain't no tree," said Mrs. Slump.

Mother's face looked as if it had stopped. "No tree?" she said. "No tree? How can we have a Christmas tree without a tree?"

"There isn't money enough," said Mrs. Guare. "We have thought and thought. There isn't money. We can buy candy, but that is all. We can't ask people to give more than they have given. I can't give more. It is the same with all of us. No crops—" Her voice trailed off.

Mother looked through the window toward the snowy prairie. "If this were Ohio, now, or Wisconsin, we'd run out to the first hill and cut a fir tree."

"I've been figgerin'," said Mrs. Slump, "that if we could find somebody 'as got a dead peach tree they ain't burned yet, and 'ud let us have it, we could use that."

"A peach tree!" Mother's voice sounded startled.

"It 'ud be better 'n nothin'. I got some green calico off a comfort that's wore out, and we could wrap little strips around the branches, maybe, so it 'ud be green." She turned to Mrs. Guare. "Ain't they some dead trees in that east orchard of yourn?"

"There are dead trees enough," Mrs. Guare said doubtfully.

"That settles it," said Mrs. Slump. "We've got our tree, if askin's havin'."

"Very well," said mother, "we'll make it as pretty as we can. It will hold the candy, anyway, and we'll cover it with popcorn and cranberries, and plenty of tapers."

"There ain't no tapers," said Mrs. Slump.

"There will have to be," said mother, firmly. "It would be too dark."

Too dark, she said, not too *dark*. I thought she was crying, but she wasn't.

The women finished making their plans. They were to come back the next week on Thursday, to sew the candy bags; and go to the schoolhouse, Friday, to wrap the tree. They would go Friday, because it might take a long time, and they could finish the work Saturday if they needed to. They would have the program Sunday. Saturday was Christmas Day, but they would have the tree Sunday, so everyone could come. The minister would be there.

The minister came to preach at the schoolhouse whenever he wasn't some place else. When he talked he said some words round and loud, and the next words quick and short until he came to another long one. His voice made me go to sleep. Father called him the Holy Ignoramus of the Lord, and mother always said, "Henry, please don't."

Father did not come home until after the women had gone. Mother told him about the Christmas tree. Birthdays were father's but Christmas Day was usually mother's. This Christmas belonged to all of us. Father and mother had something they were happy over. Almost always, when they were happy, it was about something my sister or I had done. It wasn't about us, this time. They whispered together when we were not close to them. Father didn't hate anything about the Christmas plans except the peach tree. He kept calling that a travesty. Mother was sorry we couldn't have a real Christmas tree, but said we must do the best we could.

Father made fun of the tree until the night before Thursday when the women were coming to make the bags. That night he was in earnest and wouldn't laugh. He said it was a crime to let a child's first impression of anything be a false one. He said that for all who had never seen one before, a Christmas tree would remain forever a dead peach tree wrapped in rags. I didn't understand all he said, but I liked to listen. He talked about solar myths, and the aspiration of the human spirit, and truth being always beautiful; and falsehood ugliest when it flaunted itself as religion. He said we couldn't go to the Peach tree.

Mother stopped talking and her mouth was a straight line. I was sorry. I knew how father felt. Christmas trees seemed queer to me, too. I knew they hung Christ on one, and it seemed disrespectful, afterwards, to hang presents on them and be happy about it. Mother had a song,

When He shed His blood for me
On the cruel, bitter tree,

and when she sang it father said a poem about

The God who enfleshed, and was hung on a tree
To redeem His misdeeds by His infinite love.

My aunt in Wisconsin had a fir tree in her yard. Its needles scratched, and were bitter when I pinched them in my teeth. I thought they should have hung Christ on a tree that didn't have needles; but I thought a Christmas tree would be fun, if we tried not to remember about Christ; and I wanted to go.

Mother sent my sister Teressa and me to bed. She and father talked lower and lower. When they talked together, not laughing, I was frightened without knowing why.

What wakened me in the morning was father whistling in the kitchen. It was dark, and he had lighted a lamp. He was walking back and forth, whistling. Mother called, "Henry, are you up?" Father said, "Yes," and began whistling again. He made up the tunes he used. Mother called again, "What are you doing at this time of night?" and father said, "Tinkering around."

We had breakfast by lamplight. When it was daylight I went to the barn to see what father was doing. He was hitching up the lumber wagon. He said he was going to town. I started to run to the house, but he called me back. He told me not to tell mother he was going. I stayed at the barn, then, because there was nothing to go to the house for. Father unwrapped the lines from the brake, and jumped into the wagon. He helped me in, and we drove to the house.

Mother came to the lane, and said, "Where are you going?"
Father said, "To town."
She said, "To-day? In the wagon? What for?"
"Oh, some odds and ends."

When father wasn't answering mother he was whistling. His whistling was tuneless like wind. It had no place it needed to stop, as songs did. It went on and on.

Mother shut her lips tight. There was something she didn't say. She reached her had to me, and I jumped down.

When father had driven away, mother went into her bedroom. She stayed a long time. I began to be unhappy. I put my doll on the table and let it be just a doll. When mother came out she had her hair combed high on top of her head the way we liked it best. She caught my hands and whirled me around in a little dance we played, and said, "We will have the nicest day! We must hurry and straighten up the house, for we are going to make candy bags this afternoon. If we are through with the housework before dinner time, we can pop the corn and have it all ready to string."

We went to work. I brought cobs and filled the cob-boxes. Some winters we burned cobs, and some winters, coal. One winter we burned ears of corn, and the Slumps burned twisted hay. After I filled the cob-boxes I went to a place no one knew about except me. Until some one found me there, no one knew where to look; and no one had found me yet. I sat and listened to the wind, and to mother's and Teressa's feet. I could tell who was walking by the sound. The wind made a whistling like father's, only larger and more tired.

Four women came in the afternoon with a pail of candy. They cut bags and folded them, and mother stitched them on the machine. They put all the candy in bags tied with red gathering strings, and piled the sacks on the marble-topped table in the living room. One woman kept wondering whether they had enough, and how many sacks there were. Mother's voice sounded sharp; she said, "Go in and count them, Mrs. Crachy." Mrs. Crachy said, "Oh, no, I didn't mean that!" as if she were in a hurry, but mother made her go in and count the sacks and put down how many there were on a piece of paper.

Mrs. Slump asked mother if the younguns would leave the candy be, on the table. When mother said we would, Mrs. Crachy said, "Different with mine." Mother was annoyed. She said, "My children know better than to touch the candy, without my telling them; but if you wish me to caution them, I will." She called me to her—Teressa was sitting beside her; she had been helping make bags—and said distinctly, "The candy on the table belongs to the Sunday school. Neither of you are to touch it. Do you understand?" We both said, "Yes."

While mother was getting supper, after the women had gone, I touched each of the sacks with my forefinger. There were forty-two. One I couldn't reach without moving some of the others, so I reached in with a crochet needle to touch that.

Supper was late, because we waited for father. We ate without him, and when we were through he came. Mother put my coat on me and sent me out with the lantern when she heard the wagon in front of the house. It was dark, but I could see something long sticking out of the end of the wagon. I asked father if it was a new wagon tongue, and he said, "Yes." He unhitched the horses while I held the lantern, and we led them to the barn. He stopped at the wagon, on the way back, to get a package before we went into the kitchen. He put it on the floor in the corner, and said, "After supper," and sat down to eat. Mother asked him why he unhitched the wagon in the lane. Father said he left it there to take her to the schoolhouse in the morning. Father knew mother would not ride in the lumber wagon. He looked at her as if he wanted her to smile, and when she didn't he said he had something in the wagon to unload.

After the dishes were washed, and the table-spread put back on the table, father lifted the package from the corner and asked mother to open it. She put it on the table under the lamp. When the cover came off, the box lay full of things that shone and glittered, yards and yards of silver and gilt, shining feathery strings that I didn't know the meaning of. In one end of the box were candles. "Tapers, not candles," father corrected me. Mother said "How *like* you, Henry, to leave me all day, thinking—" She caught her breath and whispered, "I know what is in the wagon!"

"A wagon tongue," I said, jumping up and down. Father looked at me and said, "Don't be a ninny-hammer," before he turned to mother. "Yes, I bought the louts a tree. I was unwilling to have children given a false conception."

Mother put her arms around father's neck. Teressa went into the other room where it was dark. She always went away when anything was happening. If she was close enough to me she used to pinch me and say, "You little beast," to try to make me go with her.

Mother stepped back. "But, Henry, the money? You didn't go in debt for all this?"

"A trifle. A mere trifle, all of it," father began; but mother insisted, "No, really, please. I have a right to ask."

Father took an envelope from his pocket. He turned it over and over in his fingers, looking at it; then laughed and tossed it onto the table. "The whole foolishness didn't cost as much as a money order to the *Sun*. I can manage to get along without the paper for a year. I knew Dana."

Mother put her arms around his neck again. Father kept patting her back, and saying, "We'll be out of the woods, some day. We'll be out of the woods, some day." I knew he didn't mean trees.

Mother motioned me to go to bed. When she came in to see if we were asleep, I told her the joke on Mrs. Crachy about touching the candy sacks. She looked at me a long time, and then went out and looked at the bags. She called me to come and show her how I touched them. I went, in my nightgown, and showed her. She asked me if I touched any of the strings. I couldn't remember that, because I had touched them wherever it was easiest. She looked at my face a long time, again, and put me to bed.

In the morning father got up early once more, to make a standard for the Christmas tree. He said he wanted a workmanlike job done, and was afraid the Gentleman of the Cloth might handle a saw the way he handled the English language. While father worked he told me about the tree. He said it as exceptionally symmetrical, and showed me the needles, and how the branches grew. I didn't know what some of the words he used meant.

Mother would not let Teressa and me go to the schoolhouse, Friday, so we didn't see the tree again until it was trimmed. I knew how it was going to look, and it looked that way. There was a program, and we all spoke pieces. Mrs. Crachy called our names. She called on father. When she called his name some people laughed. Mother wasn't listening hard, just then, and thought Mrs. Crachy called on her; so she started up the aisle. Mrs. Slump leaned out and caught at her shawl, and whispered, "It's the mister they want, the mister!" Mother was thinking about something, and didn't notice Mrs. Slump. She drew her shawl close around her just as Mrs. Slump reached for it. When mother had spoken, the people stamped and clapped so long I didn't remember until the next day that it was father they had called on.

After the recitations were over, Claud Slump was Santa Claus. He gave everyone a sack of candy, and his sisters two. It was fun, but I was tired. As soon as the minister began to talk I leaned against father to go to sleep. He put his arm over my shoulders. I slept a long time, and when I wakened something was happening. Everything was quiet except the minister. Mother was sitting tall and straight, looking the way that made me afraid to ask questions. Father sat lower and lower on the bench, and his hand closed and opened on my arm. I looked over my shoulder to see if I could tell what was the matter. I looked as easily as I could, so mother wouldn't shake her head at me to stop. I couldn't see anything. The back of the room was dark, and faces of people sitting on high desks made white patches.

Everyone was looking toward the minister, and listening to him, so I began to listen, too. I was sorry I hadn't listened sooner, because he was almost through. He was saying: "And n o w littleboysand girls, since our e r r ingbrother has given us this b e a u tifultree, when you go home to your h o m e s to-night I want you a l l toget d o w n onyourknees, and p r a y GodthatHewill lead our e r r ingbrothertothe T R U T H."

Promises

When father talked about pulling up stakes, mother said that she would do anything if the change promised better schooling for Teressa and me. She said we had had no real instruction so far. Mother liked schools, and respected school-teachers, but father criticized them. He said what filtered through a curriculum had never yet assuaged true thirst for knowledge. Mother said common sense suggested feeding a child from a cup, instead of tossing it into the ocean to drink as best it might. Father had never attended school, because his father, who had been an instructor of Greek in Berlin, saw the emptiness of education before father was old enough to start. He had taken his family to Michigan when father was nine years old, to escape people and be close to the soil. Mother enjoyed going to college because her mother had had no chance to go.

There was something about a school-teacher written in father's copy of Tennyson's poems mother took from me when she gave me another to use. The ink was so near the color of the brown flyleaf it was hard to read. Father said it was not intended for my eyes. After I asked what it meant, father and mother discussed it at night, when I was in bed. It was *A Pledge* in father's handwriting, signed in mother's. The last of it was:

> *Now shall I give you many a son,*
> *And each trace of the old maid teacher be gone.*

Two teachers I couldn't remember had boarded with us, Miss Fletcher and Miss Montague. Father and mother spoke of both as if they liked them, so I wondered what teacher it was they wanted to be rid of. I asked mother. She said, "Let your father explain," but he only laughed, and told me to marry early, since young women, not too incased in sturdy morality, made the most pliant and amiable wives.

Teressa had gone to school more than I, because she could walk farther without being tired. Mother taught me at home. I had to learn my lessons well enough to stand by her and recite them while she listened without stopping her work. Mr. Huggins was the teacher I had gone to longest—almost a month. He was good to me, and let me play outdoors whenever I wanted to, and learn by listening to others instead of having classes of my own. Father called him the Fount of Knowledge pure and undefiled by intelligence. I liked school, except that the days were tiresome. The most interesting things happened at recess when the pupils locked Mr. Huggins in the coal shed, and on our way to and from school.

At first we went to school through the corner of our pasture and Nigger Johnson's corn patch. Father had asked him if we might, and he said yes, because we called him Mr. Johnson and were not *ornery*. I wondered what else we could call him. I knew *Nigger* was his color and not his first name. After father sued him for money he had borrowed, he would not let us walk on his land. This was the reason I stopped going to school to Mr. Huggins, because it was too far for me to walk around by the road every day.

On Wednesdays we came home by the road, to get the mail. When there were wagon tracks or hoofprints in the dust, between our cornfield and Likelys', Teressa could tell by looking closely who had made them— Indians, sometimes, or horse thieves. Once the marks showed a crazy man had been riding there. She hurried me into the corn, where we could walk without being seen, and when I began to be tired she dodged into different rows, looking from side to side and behind her. She thought we should have come to the end of the corn row long before, and believed we had gone in the wrong direction and were lost. I was so frightened I cried.

"Little silly!" she said. "Nobody but an idiot worries about being lost in a cornfield, with the road not ten feet away. Mother used to walk in *real* forests, in Ohio. I supposed you knew we were only playing a game." She picked me up and carried me.

When we came to the road I told her I had laid my Reader down where we were first lost, to mark the place.

She put me down and looked at me, and stamped her foot, and began to cry in short gasps because she was angry. "We'll be late! We'll be late! Mother will blame me—always me, and never you, though it's all your fault!" Her voice came back to me as she ran up the road. She had the book in her hand when she caught up with me again, and said she hated me, and couldn't have found it if she hadn't known how to do something I couldn't—follow our tracks in the dust.

Mother was frightened because it was late when we got home, and questioned us. We didn't tell her about walking in the corn, or about the book. Teressa and I didn't tell anyone things about ourselves and each other.

The most interesting thing I knew about school was what mother told aunt Esther while I was playing with my doll under the pantry window: *mother taught school in the schoolhouse we went to, before I was born.* Aunt Esther was visiting us because mother and Carl had visited her, and I played outdoors all day so she and mother could talk. Mother was telling her about father's buying land. It worried her to have him buy so much.

Mother was crying. I could hear her stop washing dishes and walk away from the sink to use her handkerchief.

"I taught school before Veve was born," she said. "Walked a mile, back and forth, every day, carrying Teressa in my arms most of the way . . . had her under foot all day, except when she was asleep . . . I have never told you this. I taught so I cold buy a few pretty things for my baby, and not have to use the old dresses I had been unhappy over. I had almost a hundred dollars in the bank . . . my own.

"Henry had promised not to buy more land. He was plowing what he called the *Jenkins' forty*, but I didn't suppose he had any idea of buying it. He needed a new plow, and kept saying his lack of machinery hampered him with spring work. I could see he did need another plow, but I wanted things for my baby, things I had thought about to comfort me when days were hard. I hated to give up my money. I lay awake nights, wondering whether I were being selfish. Finally, everything adjusted itself in my mind. I felt only glad I could help—not a bit reluctant, or as if I were making a sacrifice. I was as eager as he to have him have the plow."

Everything was still around me except mother's crying. I sat on my doll because she wasn't alive.

"I told him he could have the money. He glanced at me as if I were a fool, and said, 'That? That went long ago,' as if it were the most indifferent trifle in the world. I thought he hadn't understood me, and said it was my money I wanted him to use, the money in the bank. He began to laugh . . . that laugh I have learned to hate: 'I used *that* to buy the *Jenkins' forty*. Where did you suppose the money came from?'

" 'You haven't *bought* it,' I said, 'not with the money I earned for my baby, after you *promised* me—'

"He shrugged. 'What's a promise between husband and wife—in matters of business!' "

I was tired of sitting under the window where the sun was hot, and didn't like my doll. I buried her under the box elder tree where I could find her when I wanted her again, and went to the loft to look at the kittens. The black cat had seven. No one visited them except me, so they were not used to people, and opened their mouths to spit when they heard me, till I could see their tongues. But the mother cat stretched her body out long, and purred when she looked up at me. I could stroke her side, and think of other things; about school, and about things I remembered, and things I was going to know.

Glass

There was something everyone knew about except me. Mother and Teressa knew it together, and were excited but quiet, speaking in whispers as if they were frightened. Mother and father knew it, but in a different way. They did not feel alike about it, and father was annoyed because mother was uneasy. He told her nothing could disturb such preternatural felicity, but she said perfection could not last.

Father had worked so hard and fast all summer he had not talked with me as much as usual, but his eyes laughed at me as he whistled or sang. He sang words over and over under his breath, not other people's songs, but words he had read. His music stopped without ending, and began any place, like the wind. When mother said, "Henry, do rest," father would straighten his shoulders that went forward a little, and say, "Nothing tires me now, with success in sight," and go out, almost on the run, to work on the new granary. He had not supposed we would need another granary, until he saw how much wheat there was going to be. As he worked he would sing:

> "'I have cast away the tangle and the torment
> Of the years that bound my life up in a mesh,
> And the pulse begins to beat that long lay dormant—'"

He would squint his eye along the edge of a board he was planing, and finish the song in speaking words, to me: "'*And the old wounds bleed afresh,*'—only that isn't the way it is with me, now—the old hopes bloom afresh!"

I wondered why everything seemed different, and looked where
mother and Teressa did when I asked them, around me, and at the
sky. There was nothing to see. Things were stiller than usual. The trees
were still. Props stood under the peach branches to keep their heaviness
from breaking the limbs. The cottonwoods were still. Only when I came
close to them and watched a long time could I see that they moved at
all—the tops swayed, or a leaf dropped, or a grasshopper bumped into a
twig and made it twitch. The wheat stood still. It was higher than usual,
and the curved heads were yellow and fat. I didn't walk through it any
more; the beards were dry, now, and short ones underneath caught my
hair or raked my face. Besides, father had told me not to. However
long I watched, there were always places where the wheat swayed and
changed color, or a canary lighted on a stalk and made it dip.

Only the sky did not move. It had no clouds and was pale blue.
Things were so quiet I tried to think what they were like. They were
like patterns in Carl's kaleidoscope when no one turned it; like pictures
in mother's stereopticon, real but frozen; they were like glass. I made
a song about their stillness, *Everything is glass, everything is glass*, that
mother made me stop singing.

We were to begin cutting wheat. Father's binder had a flywheel, that
he had put on it one day when he was angry. He had been working in a
low place, a *draw*, which stayed wet after rain. If the horses didn't pull
hard here the binder would stop, and bundles wouldn't finish binding.
Father had to pull them out with his hands when they stuck, and
sometimes had to hook up a second team to pull the machine out of
the mud. I was riding with him on the binder, one day, when it mired
down here and a bundle stuck. He had trouble pulling it out, and
hurt his hands, and swore. It was not so wrong to swear outdoors as
in the house. He put his team in the barn, and worked in the shop
all day putting a flywheel from the corn-sheller on the binder. It kept
the bundles binding even if the machine stopped. Father wrote letters
about it, and in the spring men from the Plano company came to
look at it. They had a black box, a dynamometer, to fasten to the end
of the binder, that showed how the machine ran with the flywheel,
and without it. Father showed me long strips of paper with zigzags on
them, after the men left. They came out of the box. Some of the marks

were more irregular than others, and I asked father which were best. He was disappointed that I so failed to grasp underlying principles of mechanics. I looked at the papers again, but still couldn't be sure which was the one to be pleased about.

Father was to begin cutting grain Monday, with four binders. It was Saturday, and everything was ready, more ready than usual, for no one had anything left to do. Only one hired man needed to work, and the rest were waiting. Father decided to go to town for more binding twine. Mother did not want him to go, she wanted him to rest; but he shook his head. He could not rest, now, until the grain was in the bins. As he was ready to leave, he said I should go with him.

I was running along the onion rows, when he called me, because their blossom-balls level with my head smelled bad. I was seeing if I could run the whole length of a row without smelling them.

It bothered mother to have me go to town without first having intended to. She asked me who would tend my mocking birds while I was gone, and I said, "Teressa." The mocking birds were mine to take care of, because when Mrs. Guare made her little boy give them away, nobody wanted me to have them except me. I kept Teressa away from the cage as much as I could.

Father said I must go with him, so mother took me into the house to change my dress. She asked me if I really wanted to spend an entire day away from her, and I said yes. Father waited for me to come out, and stood holding the lines in one hand, to swing me up over the wheel. He was driving the bay colts mother didn't like to ride behind. She told him to be careful, and for us to be sure to eat something before we started home. Father laughed and said we would celebrate, but mother didn't answer.

It made me feel so unusual to be riding alone with father, that I thought how I looked sitting beside him. After he and I had talked to each other, we made rhymes about everyone at home, especially Carl and the prairie dogs. Then I pretended my feet were alive, and told father what they said to each other, and he let me drive with my hands in front of his on the lines. It was almost twenty miles to town. The day was warm, and things grew stiller and stiller except for smooth noises the buggy made, until I went to sleep.

Father wakened me turning to look over his shoulder at something behind us. He was quiet, and didn't talk any more, or make rhymes. He kept looking back, and once he stopped the colts and had me hold the lines while he turned to look. I knew we hadn't lost anything, because there was nothing in the buggy when we started but us. As we came nearer town father began driving fast. Before, he had always laughed at men who tried to drive into town as if their horses were not tired.

We went to the hitching rack in front of the store where mother would not let me take spotted beans from the barrel. Father said I could sit in the buggy while he did his errands. When he went inside the store, I climbed down to be ready to go with him the next place. Mother told us to do things once, but we didn't need to do what father mentioned unless it was important enough for him to tell us twice. As father came out, he threw some binding twine into the back of the buggy, and walked away so fast I would have had to run farther to catch up with him, if he hadn't stopped at the livery barn to tell them to feed and water his team. We went to the bank, and to Smythe Brothers' office. In both places father talked about wheat.

On the way back to the store father dropped my hand, and, shading his eyes, stood for a long time looking toward the west. "It looks bad," he said, but didn't tell me what.

When we got to the buggy father took the binding twine into the store again, and told Mr. Coulter to let it go until the next time some one was in, as we might not need it. Father looked so hungry I thought we were going to eat, now, but when I asked him he looked at me, surprised, and said, "I thought you were sitting in the buggy all this time!"

We left town driving fast. The colts grew wet and black under their harness, and salty lines of white showed on their legs. Father did not whip them. He sat leaning forward, and when they slowed up he tightened the reins and spoke low. We did not talk or make rhymes, but rode along as if I were not there, and I began to think of mother and Teressa. Father said again, "It looks bad. I'm afraid . . ." His face looked queer, and smaller than usual. I pulled at his arm: "Afraid of what?" A quick, cool wind struck our faces, and passed. After I had stopped expecting him to answer, father turned to me and said, "It's hail. In the west."

I sat as still as I could, on my own side of the buggy. It was sunny around us. I wondered why father should be afraid of hail a long way off. I had not been sure, before, that anything frightened men. I remembered all I had heard women say of hail, that it made horses run away, and sometimes killed chickens. Perhaps father was worried for me; I had on my new dress: I moved as close to him as I could, and whispered, "If it hails we can unhitch the colts, and crawl under the buggy." I had heard hired men tell of doing this.

Father looked as if he were seeing me for the first time, moved his hand to brush something away from the air, said "Child, child!" with a choking sound, and pushed me from him. He turned his back to me and told me to look out of my own side of the buggy.

The roads began to be wet. I watched lumps of mud fall back into the buggy tracks, and when I leaned from the seat and looked down, the grass and sand and water made sliding lines under me, like ridges. We stopped at a river I did not remember seeing in the morning, while father gave me the lines to hold and got out to look for the bridge. He thought it might be under water, but it had washed away. We would have to go to another crossing. Father said I couldn't remember the river, because in the morning there had been a bridge and no river, and now there was a river and no bridge.

The colts didn't want to take the strange road, and kept trying to turn back. Their twisting, and the mud and water, made us drive slower and slower. The sun slanted in my eyes, until I closed them. I dreamed things that seemed part of the day, and part of other days that had frightened me; that I was in the cherry orchard at dusk watching a cat bigger than I creep toward me, as I had seen our yellow cat creep toward birds; and that a little man, like Quilp, with sickles on his feet, tried to mow my ankles.

When I wakened, I wasn't sure whether things around me were real, or part of my dream. It was twilight, and the horses were standing still. All around was water, sheets of gray, through which grass-tufts stuck up. In front of us was water, as far as I could look, and under the horses' heads a river swirled and sucked. As I opened my eyes, father rose to his feet, and began to lash the colts with his whip. They reared and crowded the buggy back, but would not go forward. A man came running, shouting that the bridge was out, and I saw we were in a corral near a house. The man came to the side of the buggy, caught father's elbow and took the whip from his hand, before he could make father turn or listen. Father insisted that we could cross, but the man said it was out of the question. As they talked, father sank heavily into his seat, dropping his hands between his knees. The man took the lines from father, and cramped the buggy for us to get out. He was *Matson*, he said; this was Bert Matson's place; we must come in and stay at the house for the night. Father said he must get home. The colts stood with their heads hanging low, not moving their feet and twisting, as they usually did when they had to wait. After a silence Mr. Matson said, "Try Turner's crossing."

"I did," father answered. "This is the fourth bridge I've found gone."

I knew, then, I had been sleeping a long time.

Father climbed down as though he were tired, and forgot to take me along. Mr. Matson lifted me from the seat and said, "Run to your paw."

The people in the house were eating supper. Their fried potatoes smelled good. Father would not sit at the table and would not eat. When he said, "I am not hungry," I thought he meant for me not to eat, either, so I said, "No, thank you," when people passed me dishes. Mrs. Matson asked me if I were not hungry, and I said yes. She called again to father, "You better come. Your little girl is afraid to eat without you."

Father looked at her, then at me, and said, "Eat, my child. Eat if you wish."

The potatoes tasted good, because we had had no dinner.

Mrs. Matson asked if I were afraid, being away from my mother. I said, no, it was fun to do things for the first time. She said, "Well, I'm sure *my* little girl wouldn't want to be away from me. You'd be afraid, wouldn't you, Jessie?"

Jessie said, "No, I wouldn't," and Mrs. Matson told her not to try to show off just because somebody else did.

I didn't like Mrs. Matson. She stopped talking, except to tell Jessie to take me upstairs to bed when I had finished eating. It was the first time I had been in a house with stairs.

In the morning father was in a hurry to leave. He drank a cup of coffee, standing, while I finished my breakfast. The river was lower, now, and we drove to a place Mr. Matson said we could ford. I was frightened, and so were the colts, but father wasn't.

Father talked to me after we were on the road, and showed me that different plants had different types of roots, and how deep some grew, along gullies that the storm had washed out. He showed me layers of soil, and told me how each had been formed. There had been rain, he said, but no hail where we were driving; and when I asked how he could tell, he answered that I would be able to discern for myself when we came into the hail belt.

It was sunny, not warm, and a wind blew my hair back from my face. Everything was wet, but shining, not gray as it had been the night before. Once father smiled at me and said, "The flywheel may pull me out of the mire, yet." I asked if it would be too wet to cut wheat, and he said, "Not for all I have to cut."

I did not understand.

We began to pass places with the grass lying flat. We met one team, whose driver was hurrying them. He hardly drew up as father shouted, "How bad?" but called, "Everything," over his shoulder, and whipped his horses again. Father chuckled. It was the first time he had laughed since we left town. He said Jenkins was trying to travel faster than bad news; that he was hurrying to the bank to borrow money on his crop.

When we were nearer home, driving on our own land, father pointed out evidences of the storm. There had been not only hail, he said, but a terrific rain. The wheat lay flat, in great shining lakes, the stalks showing their entire length. We drove up the lane under the cottonwoods, through leaves thick along the road. The trees were slashed and ragged, and hard, green peaches from the orchard were heaped around them.

Mother did not come to meet us. Father lifted me down, in front of the house, and drove to the shed to unhitch the team. Mother came from her bedroom as I opened the kitchen door. She was sleeping, she said, because she had been awake all night worrying about us. She took off my hat, and asked me where we had been; and I told her all we had done, and that we didn't have anything to eat in town.

When she saw father leave the barn, she said, "Go, now. Run outdoors and play."

I went to the garden. At first I could not think what made it different than I remembered it, until I thought of onion smell and saw there were no onion rows. Their place was empty. Mother had gathered them, I supposed, when she saw it was going to hail; but later she was provoked when I asked her where they were.

At supper time mother told us how the hailstones had piled up around the door. She had scooped up pailfuls to cool the milk tank; some were great, irregular lumps of ice, like glass, larger than she could get into the quart measure. There were still bits of ice floating in the tank, and hailstones lay heaped in the northeast angles of buildings. The hired men had stayed at the barn during the storm. One had seen it coming, he said, and got under cover just in time. We talked of nothing but the hail.

It was not until I was in bed that I remembered my mocking birds. I got up to tell mother I would look at them, but she said they would be asleep, and not to disturb them until morning.

In the morning I went early to feed them, but the cage wasn't where it usually hung. I asked mother where my birds were. She took me on her lap and said, "I have something to tell you." As soon as father and I had left for town, Teressa had bathed my birds and hung them on the porch to dry. She did not mean to forget them, but hadn't thought of them again until after the hailstorm. One was dead.

"I kept it for you," mother said. "I put it in a little box, so you could make a little grave for it where you want it to be."

I asked why she didn't put it in the stove. Father always burned up rats and mice that he caught.

She set me down from her lap and said she had supposed I would want to see the little bird I had cared for so much; or she would certainly have disposed of it at once.

Mother had something else to ask me that I needn't answer right away: she wanted me to let the other bird go. It would be lonely without its mate, and with winter coming on I wouldn't be able to find grasshoppers to feed it. It would be happier if I let it free to fly south with other birds. It might remember where it had lived, and come back to sing for us. It would sit in the box elder trees and sing. Perhaps it would remember me enough so I could feed it. She didn't ask me to decide right away; I could think over what she wanted me to do, and tell her when I had made up my mind.

I was angry at Teressa for bathing my birds. She had always wanted to, but couldn't when I was there to keep her from it. I thought she should have kept herself from it when I was gone. The live bird would make me think of the dead one more than of itself, so I told mother she could let it go. I did not see either of them, or the cage, after the hail.

One day when I was remembering the birds, I asked father if he thought the live one would come back in the summer. He thought it very unlikely that the bird would survive more than a day or so of freedom. It had had no use of its wings, and no experience in providing food for itself. If it did, by instinct, secure food, it would still fall easy prey to any enemy.

I could see that what father said must be so, and was sorry I had kept the mocking birds shut up. He said he knew that I had caged them innocently; and had felt sure I would understand, some time, that only ignorance or depravity could find pleasure in denying any life its full development in liberty, or see beauty in what was unnatural and confined.

Father was working on machinery in the barn-shed while we talked. I went up to the loft. There was no new hay there. I thought how the hail had beaten around my birds' cage. Knowing my mocking birds were gone entirely, and that I would never have them again, either of them, helped me understand why everyone felt serious about the hail.

The Corn Knife

Father and Mr. Slump were the only ones who didn't cry when they talked about being hailed out. Mr. Slump hadn't planted any grain that spring. He said, "I didn't aim to raise no crops this year, 'cause I figgered a man can't lose nothin' he ain't got." I hadn't supposed until then that Mr. Slump planned ahead what would be best to do. At first mother was happier after the storm than she had been before. She had felt something was sure to happen, and it was a relief to have it over and done with, and everything ended. Father rode over the fields to see how badly the hail had damaged them. When he came back he paid the hired men and let them go, sent word to the threshing crew not to come, and began to take down machinery, storing it in the new granary.

A few days later he went to town alone. Mother watched for him from early in the afternoon, and sent us to the bend in the road to see if he had come in sight. Often, when he went to Wichita, he came home late, and mother and Teressa and I sat up waiting for him. We would go to the road, in the dark, to listen; and the others would laugh because I put my ear to the grass to see if I could hear his horses' hoofs. We would look at the stars, and feel the warm air on our throats, and hear crickets sing while we waited. Then mother would take our hands again, and turn back to the house. If we went inside she would rock me on her lap while she sang to us or told us poems. There was one poem that frightened me, about a cat that had stolen a woman's baby to have it for a kitten. I had stopped supposing it was Teressa she stole, but the poem still scared me because it had frightened me before. Sometimes we didn't go into the house, but sat on the step at the kitchen porch, watching the Milky Way, or northern lights under the Big Dipper. Carl and the hired men would be in bed, and when father came he would call them sleepyheaded louts for not staying up to take care of his team. Mother said growing boys needed sleep.

This time father came home before dark. We went to meet him as he drove up, and he threw the lines to Carl almost before the horses stopped, jumping down from the buggy seat as if he were happy, with a little song under his breath as we followed him into the kitchen. Mother looked at him, waiting for him to talk. He didn't speak. He was teasing her. She stood farther from him, and asked, "Did you go to the bank?"

He nodded. Mother waited again, as if speaking was hard. "Would they . . . ?"

"They can do nothing," father answered. Still his eyes shone.

"Did you see the Smythes?"

Father's eyes stopped laughing. "Yes, and they were inclined to be nasty. They said they had gone as far as they could, and altogether too far already. I told them what I was willing to do, and gave them their chance. They wouldn't take it, so now they must look out for themselves."

"*Their* chance?" mother's voice was low. "What will they do?"

"Foreclose."

"What will we be able to save?"

"I told them to take everything—a clean sweep; that I would quibble over no exemptions." Father's eyes were dancing now. He handed mother a letter from the coat on his arm. Her face was more tired as she read, than when she had been watching for him to come. She dropped into a chair, and laying her head on the table began to cry. It made father uncomfortable. "Keep a stiff upper lip," he said. "We will soon be out of the woods. Such news should bring no tears!" He patted her shoulder. Teressa shoved against me and told me to come and help carry in a box of cobs. She would not answer my questions then, but that night after we were in bed she told me father had been granted a patent on his flywheel, and hoped the Plano company was going to use it. He was going to Kansas City very soon to find out, and after a while we would go there to live. She did not tell me why mother felt bad.

That was the only time I had seen mother cry since the hail, except when she was sorry for some one else who was crying. Women came to borrow things, who had never come to see us before. Mrs. Jenkins came. She was the woman who put boiled eggs left from breakfast in with the fresh eggs she sold, to make the dozens come out even. Her purplish wrapper was faded gray across the shoulders, and patched with cloth like her handkerchief—"a piece of Jenkins' shirt," she said, holding it up. She wore a pair of Mr. Jenkins' old shoes, too, and lifted her dress to show she had no stockings.

"I ain't got drawers on," she said. "The children ain't had shoes these two years, nor I a bar of soap to wash dishes with I don't know when."

I remembered that the Jenkins children came to school barefoot, except when their feet were wrapped in horse-blanket on cold days.

Mother gave Mrs. Jenkins some homemade soap colored with streaks of bluing. We wouldn't need it, now, since the threshing crew wasn't coming, and we were going away. We said *cake* of soap, and when Mrs. Jenkins said *bar* I thought she was saying *barrel* until I asked mother.

Mr. Jenkins stopped at the house on his way from town, and cried too. Mother was displeased because father laughed: "Jenkins went into town driving fast, but he came out driving slow and singing small!" Mother's eyes were dark, and she called father arrogant. Mr. Jenkins sat at the table eating lunch mother had prepared for him, telling her how the bank had refused him money, and wiping his nose with a red handkerchief as he talked. He drew his hand across his face always in the same direction, and his nose slanted that way. I wondered if wiping it were the reason, and would have asked, but mother told me to bring Mr. Jenkins a drink of water and then go outdoors without speaking, so I wouldn't interrupt their conversation.

The neighbor women cried over something else, that wasn't hail, yet seemed part of it, as being without my mocking birds did. Father had gone to Wichita to arrange for his ticket to Kansas City, and attend to other business, and would not come home until the next morning. We had finished supper, and because he was away were sitting at the table in the half-darkness, without lamps. Mrs. Likely appeared in the kitchen doorway. She did not rap, but stood twisting her hands, saying over and over, "The corn knife's gone."

She wore no hat, and her face was all one color except where her eyes made dark hollows. Her hair was pulled back tight from her forehead, and her cheeks were sunken and thin. Mother tried to draw her farther into the room, to offer her a seat, but she pulled toward the door, making choking noises and saying, "The corn knife's gone, and I know he's went and done it. He said he would, and now he has."

Listening to Mrs. Likely made my hands cold, and my heart beat until it was hard for me to swallow, though I couldn't understand why she was so inconvenienced by losing the corn knife, or why anyone should want to take it. I waited for mother to offer her ours without being asked.

Mr. Likely had left the house before supper time, and not come back.

"He said he wanted to milk before he eat," Mrs. Likely told mother, "and a little later I seen him by the cow barn grinding the corn knife. I think to myself why anybody needed a corn knife with the crop all hailed under. I came near calling him then."

She had waited until nearly dark, and gone to look for him. The cows had not been milked, and she couldn't find the corn knife any place. Mr. Likely didn't answer when she called. He was in the corn, she thought, "hidden, or worse. Hidden, maybe, for he got to saying, after the hail, if he did it to hisself he'd do it to me, too."

Mother told Carl to saddle a horse and go to Slump's for help, while she walked home with Mrs. Likely. It was three miles to Likely's house, and I wondered how she could walk so far. It frightened me to stay in the house with only Teressa; but mother said we must stay where we were, and go to bed as soon as the supper dishes were washed.

Teressa slept with me. After we were in bed she told me Mr. Likely had gone crazy and cut his throat. It gaped wide open, but he wasn't dead. He could still walk. He could run. He was running toward us, and would reach our house just as mother and Mrs. Likely got farthest away, at theirs. She sat up in bed to listen, and the moon shone on her face as she turned toward me talking in whispers.

I wanted to close the window and door; but she said, no, if Mr. Likely came to the window we could get out through the door, and if he came to the door we could get out through the window. They must both stay open. I asked which place she thought he would come, and she said, "The window—because he's crazy."

I thought I heard her laughing, but she said it was only my imagination.

She caught my arm. "There! He just raised his head above the sill. I can see his throat!"

I looked, but he had dodged back. I looked a great many times when Teressa saw him, but he had always drawn his head below the sill.

Teressa said, "Go to sleep, baby. I'll take care of you, little idiot," and put her arms around me. "The only reason I want the window open is so it won't be hot, and make my head ache. You knew I was only pretending to see things, didn't you?"

Mother stayed away all night. Mrs. Slump stopped, in the morning on her way home, to tell us mother wanted father to come for her in the buggy as soon as he came from town. They had found Mr. Likely. He was in the cornfield, with the corn knife beside him. He had cut his throat, *cut it terrible*, Mrs. Slump said, "so bad that when they try to make him drink his swaller leaks."

Before she drove away I asked her something I had wondered about. She threw her head back and laughed before she answered me: "Ain't children the beatin'est? She wants to know if anybody remembered to take Mrs. Likely the corn knife!" She was fat, and spread over the end of the high wagon seat as she leaned over: "Yes, they took her the corn knife, and she put it in her b'u'r drawer without wipin' off, in case Likely don't get well. If he does, she'll have it to show him."

Mother was more indignant with father for laughing at the Likelys than for laughing at Mr. Jenkins. She said the accident of success had made him insufferable. Mrs. Likely was worried for fear, if Mr. Likely got well, he would be arrested and put in jail for trying to commit suicide. Father said he was not derisive of the Likelys' adversity, though severing one's jugular vein was not a sound application of intelligence to an economic problem, nor a corn knife an aesthetic medium of approach to Pluto's realm; but he was not unwilling to laugh at the absurdity of a law that punished failure in an undertaking whose success precluded punishment.

I dreamed about Mr. Likely every night, seeing him come toward me between rows of corn, his head hanging back, a wedge-shaped dark space in his throat.

The Horn

Mother gave me my Christmas present more impressively than she distributed the others'. I knew from her manner it was more important. She called me into the bedroom where only Teressa was, and took if from a box. It was a horn. The other children had horns, too, but theirs made only one noise. They could blow them one way, and make one sound. Carl's trumpet was red, and Teressa's green. Father told me the way they shone was iridescence. Both were iridescent, so they were like relations.

My horn was different. It was of white wood, slender and shiny, with four silver keys on each side. It was mother's gift. Father was not interested in it, but mother told me it was lovely. When she said it was basswood father hunched up his shoulders and laughed.

Mother wanted me to learn music. She took the horn out of the box and showed me how to hold it. She put her fingers on the keys and held the horn up with her thumbs. She played a tune on it, *Happy Land*, and went back to correct mistakes. I could hardly wait to take the horn. I wanted it so I trembled. I wanted to play something real on it. The sounds mother made were not pretty, because she was only showing me how it worked. I wanted to take it to a place alone, and play music from inside me.

When mother handed me the horn I started away with it. She caught my arm, and told me to play. She put my fingers on the keys and said, "Blow!" The sounds I made were just like hers. She told me if I got the mouthpiece wet it would split; to press it against my lips, and not put it in my mouth. Then she let me go.

The moment I saw the horn it meant more to me than anything I had ever had. I decided to keep it away from Teressa.

The day after Christmas I asked to play outdoors. Mother bundled me up because it was cold; but when I took my horn from the box she made me put it back. She said it was not a thing to be playing with in the snow. I told her I would stand in the sun and blow it, but she said my fingers would freeze stiff, I would drop it in the snow, and run off and forget it. I had to wait for warm days to take it outdoors when mother didn't notice me.

The first time I had the horn outside, I ran to the hayloft and opened the big door on the side farthest from the house. I stood looking over the pasture and began to play. I couldn't make the horn sound right. It wasn't good to make music with, but beautiful to make music through. I could play all the things that were not so with it. I played standing on top of the windmill and seeing the whole world. I played wind blowing over grain fields. I played things I had no words for; and other things that made me laugh, like father and mother leaving me at home when I wanted to go to town with them, and having to come back and get me because they remembered I needed shoes.

I did not press the keys when I played alone. I swung the horn from side to side, so all directions could hear the music I was thinking.

Every day I took the horn from the box and carried it with me. I kept it in the box as mother had told me, so it would stay clean.

Teressa and mother talked about me when they thought I did not hear, when I was playing under the window, or in the house not listening. The things they said were usually not so. I did not tell them this because it would not have been polite; and they might have stopped talking.

Teressa said, "I wonder why Veve takes that horn with her. She never plays it."

"She probably plays on it when she is out of hearing," mother said. "She must be practicing something to surprise us."

I made music with the horn a long time before they began to ask me about it. The horn was real to me, like myself. It was more real than people were, except father. Mother began telling me to play something for her. She asked me, then she insisted. She scolded me. I played *Happy Land*. I didn't like to really play the horn because it sounded ugly. Mother was disappointed because I hadn't learned to play other things. She had thought I would love the horn, and wished she had given it to Teressa.

All the time she talked I cried, but not on the outside. I was crying about the horn, and not about myself.

When Teressa wanted to be hateful she borrowed the horn. I didn't dare not let her have it, because she might tell mother. She blew it and made it squawk. When I cried because she kept it too long, mother said she had not supposed I was so selfish. It made threads of pain on the inside of my arms and legs when Teressa had the horn, and when she laid it down I would take it to the pump and wash it before putting it away. I washed it until it began to be not shiny, and the mouthpiece had black lines on it.

Because they watched and questioned me, and Teressa tried to spy on me when I carried the horn outside, I began to leave it in the house, and sit thinking about it instead. I could make music whenever I listened, and would sit in the haymow, or on the sloping roof of the machine shed with sound sweeping around me. Afterward I would throw myself face down and cry until I was hungry; and go in to supper.

We had a mortgage. When people had mortgages they had sales, and went away. We had had a sale, and were leaving. Mother was sorting things to take with us, and rooms were being emptied and boxes filled.

The bustle and stir delighted me, and the air of something unusual going on. The boxes were good to climb and jump off from. There were things mother did not pack, a statue of two lovers kissing, and an inlaid cabinet. She said father should pack those. My doll was packed. My horn still lay in its box on the bureau. The bureau cover was gone, so I was afraid mother had forgotten the horn. I took it from its box, and laid it on the table where she would see it. I didn't speak to her about it, because it was hard to make her hear me any more; I had to say things over and over before she listened.

People visited us who hadn't come before, because we were going away. Mother gave them things. Mrs. Slump came, with Clubby. I was not at the house when they drove up, but heard a noise that made me run in. Clubby had my horn. I stood by mother's chair and whispered to her that he had it. She said, "Sh!"

I went to the pantry and made a noise as if I had dropped something. When mother came to see what it was, I said, "Clubby has my horn." Mother took my arm and shook it. "I'd be ashamed," she said; "I never knew you to be so selfish and disagreeable about anything as you have been about that horn. You won't learn to play on it yourself, and you don't want anyone else to. Don't let me hear another word."

All the time Mrs. Slump stayed, Clubby played the horn. He made dreadful noises with it, and put it too far in his mouth. Mother went twice to look at the clock, and Mrs. Slump said she must go. She told Clubby to put the horn back on the table. He held it close to him and began to run. When she caught him, he kicked her. Mother said, "Let him keep it. Veve doesn't care for it any more."

They drove down the road with Clubby on the high wagon seat beside his mother, looking back and making blasts on the horn.

I cried until mother was afraid I would be sick. She talked to me. She scolded. She argued. She appealed to my pride. She asked me if I wasn't glad to have Clubby have one little gift, poor Clubby who had so little. I was not. To every question I had one answer, "It was mine, and you gave it away." She reminded me that father always sold our pigs and colts and baby heifers. I answered, "This was really mine."

"I'd be ashamed," she ended, "to make such a fuss over a wretched horn that didn't amount to anything in the first place."

"You *told* me it was lovely."

Long after the rest of the household were in bed, father held me in his arms in the empty kitchen. He gave my grief a name and made it less. The horn was a symbol, he said, and the human spirit clung to symbols. Only the wise saw the reality behind the sign. He had not wanted me to have the horn, he said, but he had had faith in me to believe it would not corrupt me. By degrees he made me bigger than my loss.

The next day mother took time she couldn't spare (she said) to sit in her rocking-chair and hold me on her lap. She told me she had been wrong when she gave away my horn without asking my permission; but if she had asked me to let Clubby have it, she would have expected me to say yes. She would have felt shamed and embarrassed if I had refused. She hoped, when so much worried her, that I would make things easier for her, instead of harder.

I settled lower on her shoulder and said, "Talk more."

She told me why Christmas presents were lovely. No matter how small they were, how inexpensive, they were lovely. The affection that prompted them was beautiful. The sacrifice that bought them, the joy they gave—all, all were lovely, regardless of the gift.

She rocked me in silence.

I remembered more and more that the end of the horn had begun to have tiny black lines on it, and tried to believe I had wanted to give it away.

A Pine Tree

As soon as father had found a house for us in Kansas City, and told Carl to go to school, he left; the Plano company needed him in another place. He was to take charge of an exhibit of their machinery, and could come home only for a day or night once in two or three weeks.

Carl attended high school in a different building and a different direction than Teressa and I, so we were with him very little. Even at night I hardly saw him, since he was always on the street or at the drug store with Leo Reinhart or other boys bigger than he. Mother did not like Leo.

It was after Christmas before we were ready to start school, near the end of the term, so mother went with Teressa and me to the principal's office to see if we might enroll. Teressa had a report card. We knew where she belonged, but I had studied at home. Mr. Terrill heard me read, and said, "Her reading is all right." He asked me questions in arithmetic that were so easy I didn't answer until I had looked toward mother; he said, "Her arithmetic is all right." Then he pointed to a sentence in a Reader, and asked me what part of speech it was. I answered that there were so many words I didn't know what part it would be. He tapped his pencil on the word *house*, and said, "I am not asking about the whole sentence, I am asking about this . . . one . . . *word.*"

I thought of all the languages there must be, and knew one word couldn't be a very big part. I said, "A millionth, maybe?"

Mother looked as though I had bothered her. She said I hadn't studied technical grammar yet, but she hoped even so Teressa and I might be assigned to a room together. I was sorry she did, because I had hoped we wouldn't be. Teressa wanted me not to spend time with anyone but her, but I liked other children.

Mr. Terrill put us both in Miss Helm's room. Miss Helm was little and dark, and wore a green silk dress. The children thought she was cross, but she was nice to us after the first few days. We sat in a double seat, and Miss Helm was sorry we had only one set of books. The third day we were in school, she asked us to stay after the rest left, and told us we must not whisper—that I must not, for Teressa didn't except when I made her. I said I didn't whisper; I explained that I was only speaking to Teressa, who was my sister. Miss Helm stopping frowning at me and smiled, and said she knew Teressa was my sister, and that I must stop speaking to Teressa my sister during school hours.

We had been in Miss Helm's room only three weeks when the class was promoted to Miss Wilson's room. Just before we were promoted, Miss Helm asked us to remain after school again, to tell us Miss Wilson had complained that we whispered to each other while we were standing in line to be dismissed. She wanted us to get along well in Miss Wilson's room, and wanted Miss Wilson to like us; and she was sure Miss Wilson would be better pleased if we were careful not to talk.

I did not speak to anyone in the new room. Miss Wilson was particular about everything, so we did wrong without knowing it until she began to punish us for what we were doing. She hit my hands with the pointer during writing lessons, but that was because I sat on the front seat nearest her.

There was one set of lessons that she drilled us on over and over, until we knew them by heart. Pupils who had been in her room before said these were the lessons we would recite when Mr. Greenwood visited us. Mr. Greenwood was the city superintendent. If a boy from the room below us came in and laid a Music Reader on the desk without saying anything, Miss Wilson would send the book on to the next room, and begin on those lessons. We would be reciting them when Mr. Greenwood came in.

One of the definitions she drilled us on in mental arithmetic was *weight: Weight is the force by which a body is drawn to the earth through gravity.* I said it over and over. We were reciting this when Mr. Greenwood came, early one afternoon. Miss Wilson smiled at me and asked if I could tell her what *weight* was. I had been sitting so still my arms and feet felt queer when I stood up, like glass. I began, "*Weight is the force*..."—my thoughts ran ahead—*gravity*...*gravity*...that meant *not laughing when something funny happened*...it must be the wrong word. I stopped, and began again: "*Weight is the force by which a body is drawn to the earth through gratitude.*"

A boy laughed. Teressa pinched me—hard—when I sat down. Mr. Greenwood asked if he might talk to the class, and asked us questions, not those in the lesson. He was quiet and pleasant, but some of the pupils cried because they didn't know what he wanted them to answer. I didn't hear all he said, because I was thinking about *weight*. Miss Wilson sat looking down at her desk. Her hair was soft and pretty on top of her head, as she bent over, and she did not look up until Mr. Greenwood left.

Teressa had a note from mother, asking that she be excused at recess that day because mother was sick. She pinched me again as she was taking her books from the desk to go home. After recess Miss Wilson said the class should go to the blackboard to diagram sentences. She numbered us, and gave each pupil a different sentence to write. I didn't know what *diagram* meant, so I watched to see what the others did. Each was putting the words of his sentence on lines. Some of the lines were one-sided and awkward, and I felt sure I could make mine evener than those. My sentence had eleven words, and I arranged it like a pine tree lying down, with a little word at the tip, and two words with the same number of letters at the other end for roots. I was almost the first one through when I looked around at the others, and thought my diagram was the best. Miss Wilson picked up the pointer as she came toward me. I thought she took it to point out my work; and stepped aside for the class to see it so quickly that I forgot to lay my crayon on the crayon rail. She hit me over the hands to have me lay it down, but I dropped it, and when I stooped to pick it up she hit me over the shoulders and head. She talked louder and louder, and said I had disgraced the entire class, and should never have been permitted to enter her room in the first place; I might be some other teacher's pet, but in her room I would learn to do my work, or leave.

It seemed a long time until school was dismissed. The children who walked home in the direction I did said Miss Wilson would not have touched me if Teressa had been in school. They called her sweet William. I did not eat supper that evening, and in the night I dreamed, even when I sat up in bed with my eyes open, and saw diagrams on the wall. I confused things that had happened in school with others that had happened before we came to Kansas City. Part of the time I thought I was hunting for my horn that mother gave away, to put it with things she had let me keep.

I didn't go to school with Teressa in the morning, or even get up, but stayed in bed while mother put cold cloths on my head because I had been delirious in the night.

When Teressa came from school that evening, she was crying, and her face was so swollen her eyes were almost shut. At first she could not answer mother's questions, but stood at the sink bathing her face and catching her breath. She was angry.

I hadn't told mother about my diagram being wrong, because we didn't tell her things that would worry her; but the children told Teressa the next day. When Miss Wilson asked her why I was not in school, she did not answer. Miss Wilson tried to put her arm around Teressa when she asked her the second time, and Teressa pushed it off and told her she hated her. Miss Wilson sent her to the cloakroom until she would say she was sorry, and she had stood there all day.

Miss Wilson said Teressa must apologize, but Teressa said she would never say she was sorry, because she wasn't.

Mother was astonished that Teressa had spoken so to a teacher, until Teressa told her I had been punished. She said she would go with Teressa, the next day, to see Miss Wilson; and for Teressa to stop crying, and lie down, and let mother bathe her face. Mother was more bothered, because father was coming home soon, and she wanted everything smooth.

I was still out of school when he came, and he and mother agreed that I should be outdoors playing instead of studying.

When mother told him what had happened, he sat down at once to write a letter to Miss Wilson. Mother let him read it to her, but would not let him send it. He called Miss Wilson a hellicat and a devil-begotten vixen, and said the sublime simplicity of his daughter's answer about language, when she was assailed by scholastic imbecility, was beyond a pedant's appreciation. He wanted Teressa to be taken out of school at once, and asked mother if she had used her authority to force apology from her elder daughter for speaking the truth.

Since mother would not permit Teressa to leave school, father took Carl out. He said he wanted Carl exposed to the sweet reasonableness of piston rods and cam wheels. Carl worked in a machine shop until he ran away, and only Teressa went to school.

Spring Beauties

There were vacant lots near our house, with walnut trees in sunny places where spring beauties grew. Mother had not liked the Kansas flowers, nor had time to gather them with us. Now, she would take a book or the *St. Nicholas*, and Teressa and I would go with her to one of the sunny, shady places, and sit under the trees while she read to us. I would gather short-stemmed spring beauties for her, or put my head in Teressa's lap, and sleep.

We liked to stay outside, because things were less bare outdoors than in the house. We had beds, and a stove in the kitchen; but the beds were not upstairs in the bedrooms, and it embarrassed mother to have them where they were. She wished to keep the furniture we had used on the farm, when we moved, especially her rosewood wardrobe and the mahogany beds that came from New York, but father did not want them. He was starting a new life, he said, in a new environment, and desired nothing that would remind him of the past. Mother said she could begin a new life with old furniture better than with none at all.

We had a carpet for the stairs, but it stood in a roll in the corner of the hall. It was not proper to put tacks in the floor, and father said stair rods were an abomination; we would move soon, so furnishing the house would be a waste of labor.

Father was away from home a great deal. He traveled for the Plano company, and returned only for a few days at a time, to tell us of places he had visited—wheat fields in Dakota, and redwood forests and the Soldiers' Home in California.

Mother was prettier than she had been, because she was no longer tired. When we lived in Kansas she wore her hair drawn straight back as the other women did, but her dresses were not like theirs. Neighbors who helped her during threshing laughed because she did not say: "Call the men to dinner," but always, "Call the men to dinner while I put on a clean collar," starting toward her bedroom, taking off her apron and rolling down her sleeves as she went. There she would stand in front of the mirror opposite the picture of the *Nymphs and Pan*, and smooth back her hair, take a small clean handkerchief and fold it for a collar, pinning it with a brooch at her throat. After we went to Kansas City she wore her hair soft around her face, and her new dresses made her look tall and straight.

She spent a great deal of time with us because she might be going to leave us, and held us close, telling us things to remember: always to be good to father, and for me to obey Teressa. I did not understand, at first, and it frightened me more when I thought some one might take her away, and not let her come back, than it did when Teressa told me mother was going to the hospital, and was afraid she might die.

While she was in the hospital, Teressa kept house. We had a good time, except when father came home and did something that made Teressa cry. Things he said seemed funny to me, but not to her. He told her a competent cook gauged the amount of salt she needed with her fingers; and when Teressa salted the oatmeal with her fingers, the next morning, he said it was a slovenly habit, and she should use a spoon. I laughed—not at Teressa, but because I thought she would laugh, too, and we would tease father about having said opposite things; but she cried all day, after father had gone, and pinched me when I came too near her.

On the days father took me to the hospital to see mother, I gathered spring beauties, and carried them to her in a blue glass vase he said was an eyecup. He always advised me not to take them, as they would divert my attention from matters on which he wished to converse with me. If I put them down at once when he spoke, he usually did not notice that I had them with me, until we stepped onto the street car. Once he set them on the window ledge for me, and the conductor smiled because I got almost off the car without them. Mother always felt worse after father had visited her. I did not know why. When he left us together I stroked her hair until she breathed evenly again, and fell asleep.

It was while she was away that I began to sit on the porch in the evening listening to other children play. There were ten or twelve, in the block, who played together in the twilight until their mothers called them in. One fat girl with white arms wore a soft dress that had no sleeves. Another, whom I liked best to watch, had prettier clothes than anyone, and in the daytime wore a hat with blue and yellow daisies on the brim. It was she who decided what games to play, and who should be *it*. One night she turned back as she passed the house, and climbed the terrace step toward the porch.

"Why don't you play?"

"I don't know."

"Would you like to?"

"If I knew how."

She looked at me disapprovingly. "Everyone knows how to play games." After a moment she asked, "Are you tony?"

Having never heard the word before, I didn't know.

"Ask your mother if you are tony. If you are, you can play with us."

I explained to her why mother was not at home.

"Then you must ask her as soon as she comes back, but you can play with us until you find out."

She caught my hand and ran down the sidewalk to the other children: "She is going to play with us. If she can't, I won't."

We played singing and running games, like *King William* and *Hide and Seek*. I played with them every night, Teressa sometimes looking on, until mother came home from the hospital, and said she could not permit me to run wild with children whose parents she knew nothing about.

Nothing had ever seemed so lonesome to me, not even mother's giving Clubby Slump my horn, as sitting beside her on the porch, hearing children call to each other in the soft darkness.

When the children stopped asking me why I didn't play, they began asking why we didn't have flowers in our flower bed. All the yards in the block were alike, a terraced lawn, with a flower bed in the middle. The other beds had plants in them. The emptiness in ours showed less, because the grass grew tall around it. We had no lawn mower.

It seemed especially fortunate, one afternoon when mother sent me for bread, that the grocer had none of the kind she wanted, so I could use the money for something else. I went to the florist's in the next block, and bought a feverfew in a pot, and a black pansy plant. He gave me the pansy plant.

Mother and Teressa were both provoked with me when I brought back the flowers instead of the money, and mother told me not to take things into my own hands that way again; the two plants would look ridiculous in the big bed. I told her I would care for them and water them, and perhaps they would spread.

Both grew. I was the only one who paid attention to them, and the only one who needed to say good-by to them when we moved.

A Cast Leaf

During my father's stay in Europe, and the year of his return, the variously tinged shadows hovering over earlier childhood where light had been withheld integrated themselves into a fairly comprehensive picture.

I knew, never from direct enlightenment, but from word fitted to word, comments half caught, and memories of low-voiced bitterness, that it was a stranger whom father called "*my wife*." By entries in old account books, and records in the family Bible, I knew that his children, Augusta and Carl, had been young when he and my mother married.

The circumstances of their marriage, and the gulf that opened between them almost in the moment of their union, lay wrapped in that atmosphere, exciting and impenetrable, which had stirred my childhood to pondering and question: so that I envisaged the two held in a globe of darkness, yet separated by a deeper darkness at their feet, wherein hid all that later rose between them.

I knew that Carl and Augusta had given mother their affection, and father had resented that gift, as love diverted from her he mourned; and, loving his dead wife, had almost hated her children, and dealt harshly by them, sending Augusta to her mother's people before I could clearly remember, and alienating Carl. Mother had grieved over father's injustice to his children, and remonstrated with him, but could not force her pride to direct interference between a parent and his offspring, even while she condemned herself that under her roof children were abused.

She hated the children's mother inexplicably. A single word of scorn, forcing its way with bitterness incredible on her gentle lips, bared to me the source of her aversion (that I had always sensed) for the cameos she did not wear, the lovely ring she wore only at our childish instancy, the Houdon bronze of lovers, kissing; and the strange Ailanthus trees, symbol of those planted by living lovers at their gate. Memory leaped, again, at almost invisible bronze of ink across a brown flyleaf, a bit of doggerel in my father's writing signed by mother. I read with indignation and greater astonishment; bewilderment renewed and intensified that mother and Teressa should take father seriously. He was a playfellow, to be agreed with and cajoled and outwitted; to be laughed at sometimes, and teased, and always loved.

He had left for Europe in high spirits, to introduce in Russia

The little Plano binder
With the flywheel on behind her

too elated with success to do more than promise me that I should steer his yacht on the Mediterranean, and (for cultural contacts) establish us in a frigid neighborhood.

I saw it was not having money *to spend* that made us different from other people. Mother wanted clothes, to be suitably clad on the street, to visit our teachers without embarrassment, or attend church. Father's irony suggested that if she were to be sick, during the winter, she would need little outer clothing. He added that if she delay her purchases until his return from Europe, he would bring her a fabulous garment; provoking her rare retort, that a twenty-dollar wrap was warmer than a thousand-dollar promise.

Because of her ill health while father was away, Teressa and I had less of her companionship, and tried to care for her instead of burdening her with our care. For the first time, we began to have fun she did not share. I had suddenly shot up, taller than Teressa, and stronger. She no longer pinched me. When she flew at me in nervous fury from overwork and anxiety, I held her wrists while she stormed and fumed. We began to be companionable friends, and took long walks together, sometimes visiting shops without telling mother of our adventures.

Teressa now did all the buying for the family, tormenting herself to purchase economically, that father's checks for royalties might remain intact. Mother had set her heart on accumulating a specific amount in the bank before his return. Her desire had become an obsession, a last appeal for affectionate appreciation. Because we half understood this, and from long-established acquiescence, we coöperated loyally.

Teressa was entering high school; I was two years behind her. We were with children only during school hours. One of my classmates had included us in invitations to her birthday party, early in the year. I was excited and happy. Mother fingered the invitations, her face flushing, and asked if we really cared to go. . . . I had a suitable dress, but Teressa had none . . . there would be presents. . . . She looked at us. Teressa hastily disavowed all interest, and at the suggestion of implied expense, I was too constrained to voice my own eagerness.

Mother was secretly ashamed that we had been deprived of this opportunity for companionship. For the first time she had consciously, and not of necessity, sacrificed us to the forces that dominated her. I knew it was my right to have been with other children. Teressa felt this, too, for when we had gone to bed she raged and beat her pillow, saying she wanted me to be like other girls—for herself she didn't care; she hated Clara Flynn and hated her parties.

No longer could mother entirely control Teressa in her rages. When Teressa stamped her foot, and said she hated father, and was waiting only for the time she need never see him again, mother's face would grow infinitely sad, its lines deepen, as she answered, "My dear, my eldest-born, remember he is your father." Sometimes Teressa would stop crying, and be sorry; but more often she would retort bitterly, "I shall not forget. . . . And don't imagine," she would add savagely, "that he will think any more of you because you scrimp and save until we live like freaks. He won't even know it."

Perhaps this reiterated taunt laid my mother's spirit bare to devastation when father returned. I was in the room as he unpacked excellent luggage, when mother brought forward her triumph of self-denial: "How much money do you suppose we have in the bank?"

"A trifling amount," father answered, absentmindedly.

As mother tried to open the bank book before his eyes, her hands incompetent with eagerness, he gestured it aside: "Some later time. Let us first conclude the business in hand."

The light faded from mother's face, while my very body seemed to cry to father for understanding.

He continued to unpack gifts—a carved comb from Milan; from Vienna, wistful amethysts that matched mother's ring; a curiously wrought star and crescent from Constantinople; scarfs—brooches— tapestries. Mother accepted each with polite courtesy, laid each aside a shade too promptly, till father's attention was challenged: "Is my selection not pleasing to you, my dear? Are you not gratified with my choice?"

Mother had learned, too grimly, the easy lesson of commanding attention by not extending it. The fountain of joy in her had ceased to play.

Month by month, before her apathy, Teressa's speech grew less restrained, and the more revealing to me. And, while the phrase oftenest on father's lips was, "*The child observes nothing*," I was selfconscious and uncomfortable in knowledge I was not supposed to share. I knew, now, the reason for mother's recurrent sicknesses, and that she again hoped to bear a child.

This possibility was altogether wonderful to me, like something that couldn't be happening to us—a glorious mystery, remote in golden haze. My delight held no speculation as to cause or seasons, whether the awaited baby should belong to us next week, or in a sunny moment twelve months hence; expectation was enough. But Teressa was in fury. "I hate it," she muttered as she worked, "I hate IT and I hate her. She loves IT better than she does me. All I am good for is to slave and slave, to wait on her now, and afterward on IT." I tried to draw closer to her by saying, "I know what you mean," but she turned on me with an intensity that silenced me, little as I feared her physically in my superior strength.

Father was home at irregular intervals, for a day or so at a time, and Aunt Esther had come to be with mother. Before her arrival father had brought a doctor to the house, a swarthy man, abrupt in manner, who terrified mother. Even I saw that she had a morbid horror of him, and wondered why father did not perceive this, or why mother did not insist on consulting some one else. She did protest hesitantly that she disliked the man; but father approved him highly, and spoke German with him when he called, jovially commanding more of his attention than mother received. For the first time mother turned in confidence to me, instead of to Teressa, whispering fearfully that father and the doctor *together* were inimical to her.

One morning when Teressa was in the city for errands that would consume the afternoon, Aunt Esther told me I must go for the doctor. Mother was worried over not having Teressa there to depend on, and wanted to give me instructions herself; I was to go to her room.

She was in bed when I went in, and between gasps told me how to reach the doctor's office, and go at once—by street car to save time. It was a long ride, an hour's, perhaps, by car. She took a dime from the purse under her pillow, then replaced it and handed me five cents, telling me to have the doctor start at once, and bring me back with him in his carriage. I was ill at ease, knowing I would find it impossible to suggest such an arrangement to the doctor, but too long trained in obedience to question mother's orders. She repeated that she would feel far less anxious if Teressa were going, instead of me.

I found Dr. Herron in his office. He was overbearing and surly as I gave my message, and asked roughly whether there was any hurry. I said, yes, mother had given me carfare so that I could reach him more quickly—carfare one way, I added. He eyed me sharply and said, "Well, what about it? Is there any real rush, or not?"

I said again that mother sent word for him to come to her at once, but my dry mouth would not form words to suggest that I ride back with him.

"I'll be along," he said, and walked out to his carriage, where his driver waited beside the black horses father had admired at our door.

I went out behind him, to start the long walk home.

I carried a troubled sense of inadequacy, though I had not the slightest realization of the need for haste. I knew that the doctor had no intention of hurrying, and that I had not made him understand emphatically enough. It would be hours before I could reach home.

It was early fall, and hot. Leaves from overhanging trees littered the sidewalk. I stooped, hunting perfect ones to take to mother, but each was marred, shriveled at the edge or insect-eaten at the tip. I rejected all but one crimson maple leaf. It comforted me, and I rolled its smooth stem between thumb and finger as I walked. I was exhausted long before I neared home, and sat for a moment on terrace steps to rest. A woman at the door of the residence asked what I was doing, saying steps were not made for passers-by to sit on; but as I rose she asked me if I wanted a glass of milk. A surge of unfriendliness toward her surprised me; "Like Teressa," I said to myself, and answered her shortly, as Teressa might.

Aunt Esther met me at the door, her face drawn. She plied me with questions. What had happened? Where was the doctor? Why hadn't I brought him with me? Why had I been so long? Only when she asked again and again why I had not come with him, I answered that he had started without me. For the first time, an answer of mine was in spirit consciously a lie.

Aunt Esther told me mother couldn't be bothered with leaves, now; a physician was with her.

Late that afternoon my aunt confronted Dr. Herron at the door. Her voice was beyond anger: "You are too late."

"The baby?" he questioned.

"Dead."

He started to elbow past her, asserting his responsibility to the child's father. She blocked his way: "Cross that threshold and I will kill you with my own hands!"

Aunt Esther talked long to father, when he came, before he went to mother's room. My aunt was in the kitchen preparing a tray for mother, and I was hovering outside the bedroom door in wretchedness of self-condemnation, when mother's scream rose high and uncontrolled. Aunt Esther passed me, running to the room, but father's voice came first, "It is nothing, nothing whatever." Mother's interrupted, higher and wilder, "He says it is what a man might expect from an old maid school-teacher!" Then father's voice again, deprecatingly, "Now, Augusta, now, my dear, you entirely misconstrued . . ." and my aunt's, "Leave this room, and call a doctor."

I crouched under my bedroom window, remote from mother's cries and my aunt's quieting voice. The center of my grief was that she should not know my abasement, or its bright penitential gift. I remembered a strange night when she had refused cherries I had gathered for her; but my leaf she had not even known of, to refuse.

The next night my aunt called me from bed to go to mother's room. Teressa was already dressed. To her she said, "Control yourself. Not a sound while she talks to you!" and to me, "Smile at your mother when you go into her room."

Mother's eyes were large and dark, and hungry for us. She spoke to Teressa: "I put Veve in your charge. Care for her. Guard her. I tried to make your home a happy one . . ." She took my hand, painfully, as if the effort was great: "Be happy. Stay happy, always. Remember this, both my girls: Life is a gift. It is a privilege. And no life holds so little it were better not to have lived."

Here face quivered. When it was again calm she said, "Be good to your father. Remember that he is your father, whatever happens." She motioned me to leave, and Teressa to come closer.

When Teressa came to bed she sobbed until I thought she would strangle, writhing, and clutching her hair and pillow.

I asked if mother were dying. With quick transition characteristic of her, she answered soberly: "I don't know. Probably not. It doesn't make much difference, either way. If father doesn't kill her this time, he will next. I wasn't crying about that. If you had been called to mother's bed as many times as I have, you would understand how I feel. I have been told to 'guard your little feet' until I hate your little feet. To-night, when mother said that to me again, I asked who had ever guarded mine. You have been the baby, always, until I've hated you. I've hated everything. Yet, if things could have been a *little* different for me, I might have liked them. I don't care, any more, and that was why I was crying, *because I don't care.*"

She turned heavily, with a long quivering breath: "One thing— mother says she has provided for our education. All in the world I ask is to begin earning money, so I can take you some place where we can be by ourselves, and live like human beings. . . . You knew father was buying wheat?"

Her remark seemed curiously irrelevant. I had heard father praise the hand-ground wheat of his boyhood. At worst his purchase was a troublesome whim on his part, that would give Teressa the work of grinding it in the coffee mill each morning.

No, Teressa said, he wasn't buying wheat that way. But bushels and bushels, buying it as he had bought land in Kansas.

The interior of our woodshed rose plain before me, its uneven floor and random shelving, and the gaping crevices around the window. It was an inadequate place to store grain.

He wasn't going to store it, Teressa explained more uncertainly. He wasn't buying it to take it from where it was, but to spec—

Her voice died in the middle of the word. She was asleep.

Le Bonnet Rouge

Teressa had a red hat, a gay little cheap thing that called a flush to her cheeks, and brightened her somber face. Its adventurous color must have summoned her spirit, too, and set her for the moment out of character; for I had known her only as a harassed, tigerish, affectionate big sister, my scourge and my refuge, three years my senior and already fifteen.

She was my "big" sister by courtesy only, for my blond head over-topped her dark one by two inches, and at times my dignity seemed older than her darting eagerness.

On this day of high adventure, when the little hat seduced her, household matters had moved with unwonted smoothness. Teressa had risen early and done the washing; had baked and scrubbed and prepared lunch—with little help from me, probably, for she cherished a mysterious conviction belied by life that I was not meant for such tasks. She had slipped through the day without the crises of nervous fury brought on by overwork, which often dragged everyone around her into a vortex of emotional high pressure.

Three o'clock came. The work was done, and Teressa was serene.

"Now," she said, "I will hurry and dress and we can take a walk."

Occasional strolls together were the delight of our hearts. These walks had only one drawback. Teressa's preoccupations made her negligent of hairpins, hatpins, and the security of petticoats. At any moment when we were together on the street, my snug barette might be commandeered to anchor a swart queue rolling unexpectedly down her back. My hatpins were at the mercy of her necessities; and all too often, with shame in my cheeks. I had been called on to pin up her ruffles in public. This was a double bitterness to me, because both disposition and leisure gave me to the street groomed and impeccable; but my sarcasm availed nothing against her miserable habits.

She had been at her "dressing" but a moment when she emerged for the street, her jaunty hat a bit askew, and an air of unusual competence upon her.

"Did you remember your garters?" I asked anxiously.

"Certainly. You needn't be hateful!"

I held my breath, fearful for the fragile joy of the day; but she had not taken offense, and we were off.

"Where are we going?"

"A new place," Teressa answered, with a finality that forbade questions.

We trotted along, Teressa's animated face upturned to mine, while she expounded to me the marvel of the sun that is Sirius. (Against our childhood wrongs I set this, that our casual family conversation never descended to the level of our neighbors' clotheslines!) Suddenly—puff!—a gust of wind lifted the little hat and set it lightly beyond a picket fence.

The fence pales were too close set for us to crawl through, and too sharp to climb. At last we found a stick, and with much patient leaning and fishing recovered the truant bonnet. Teressa examined it tenderly and found it unhurt.

"Give me a hatpin," she demanded.

For once I rebelled. I had only one pin in my own hat. I expostulated. I argued. Why was it worse for her to lose her hat than for me to lose mine?

"Yours is old, and mine is new," she countered.

"Hold on to it, then!" I retorted.

"I guess I'll have to," she agreed, "but my arms are tireder than yours."

There was justice in that, and my conscience stung me as we went on. To shake off discomfort I asked again, "Where are we going?"

"We are going to dine at Blaker's restaurant," she answered impressively.

The splendor of her language, even more than the splendor of the undertaking, awed me. After a time I whispered, "Have you money?"

"I have," she answered firmly; and opening her water-reddened little claw she disclosed a quarter. I had noted before, with disapproval, that her right hand was tightly clutched, but attributed its grip to her handkerchief, which she always carried rolled in the smallest possible compass, having no flair for a gesture or a flourish.

We reached the restaurant, and paused for an instant before Teressa plunged through the swinging door. Behind her, I grew conscious of a dazzling blur of mirrors, napery, and silver; and then the quiet-stepping waitress was seating us.

Teressa settled herself with determined composure, and laid all her cards on the table in the shape of one moist coin. "If we both have soup will it be more than a quarter?"

"It will be twenty cents," the waitress answered. There was something indefinably sympathetic and reassuring about her voice.

It was not an hour for fashionable dining. Only two guests, across the room, leaned at leisure and gave their attention to each other. The solitude, the kindly waiter, the certainty of ample funds gave us aplomb.

Soon we were chatting happily over the soup. Teressa suggested that if we knew all—all—about any one thing we would necessarily know all about everything. I demurred, and she insisted. "We would, we would," she repeated vehemently; and at her final nod—plop!—the little red demon of a hat plumped itself upside down in her plate of soup.

Sickness of mortification rolled over me in waves. I saw her incredulous horror as, spoon suspended, she gazed into a cavernous lining of black sateen. My eyes turned to see if others were watching, and my chagrin was swept away in indignation. The two across the room were laughing! Laughing—at my dear sister—when she was in trouble! She must not see them!

Quietly I reached across the table and lifted the dripping hat, smiling as I did so into her tragic eyes. "I *wanted* that soup! I *wanted* that soup!" she wailed.

Even as she spoke the gentle waitress was at our table, leaning deferentially at Teressa's elbow. "I shall bring Madame another plate of soup. There will be no charge—and let me brush Madame's hat and hang it by the mirror, where she can see easily to put it on."

Oh, blessed understanding of a child's heart! Magic solace of the word *Madame!* No *Madame* need let hot tears roll down her angry cheeks! Tears and flush receded. "Madame" was herself again.

As our gracious waitress placed the second service, Teressa said earnestly: "We have a nickel left. On the way home I shall invest in a hatpin."

CPSIA information can be obtained
at www.ICGtesting.com
Printed in the USA
LVOW04s2034241115
464045LV00016B/81/P